A Frosty COMBINATION

A Tea & Sympathy Mystery

BOOK 5

J. NEW

A Frosty Combination
A Tea & Sympathy Mystery
Book 5

Copyright © J. New 2021

The right of J. New to be identified as the author of this work has been asserted in accordance with the Copyright, Designs and Patents Act 1988. All rights reserved. No part of this publication may be reproduced, stored in or transmitted into any retrieval system, in any form, or by any means (electronic, mechanical, photocopying, recording or otherwise) without the prior written permission of the publisher. Any person who does any unauthorised act in relation to this publication may be liable to criminal prosecution and civil claims for damages.

This is a work of fiction. Names, characters, businesses, places, events and incidents are either the products of the author's imagination or used in a fictitious manner. Any resemblance to actual persons, living or dead, or actual events is purely coincidental.

Cover design: J. New.
Interior formatting: Alt 19 Creative

Other Books By J. New

The Yellow Cottage Vintage Mysteries in order:
The Yellow Cottage Mystery (Free)
An Accidental Murder
The Curse of Arundel Hall
A Clerical Error
The Riviera Affair
A Double Life

The Finch & Fischer Mysteries in order:
Decked in the Hall
Death at the Duck Pond
Battered to Death

Tea & Sympathy Mysteries in order:
Tea & Sympathy
A Deadly Solution
Tiffin & Tragedy
A Bitter Bouquet
A Frosty Combination

Chapter One

THERE WAS A distinct chill in the air as Lilly Tweed, former agony aunt, now purveyor of fine teas, cycled through the park of her home town Plumpton Mallet. Autumn was just about holding on by a thread, as winter was beginning to make its presence known. Usually her cat, Earl Grey, would ride in his carrier in the bike's basket, but this evening he was snuggled in the large front pocket of her jumper, as his usual place was in use. She'd purchased the sweater specifically for the festive season because it was designed to carry your favourite pet as well as being a holiday design. Whenever the cat stuck his head out of the faux fur-lined pocket sewn around her midsection, he appeared to be wearing an elf hat and ears.

In the basket, Lilly had positioned a picnic hamper filled with buffet food. She was pushing her luck a bit, choosing to cycle rather than drive, but the weather, although chilly, was showing the last few rays of sunshine and she loved riding in it. It would probably be the last chance she would get before winter set in properly and she was forced to relegate the bike to the shed until spring.

As she slowed down and eventually stopped at the rear of her shop premises, she breathed a sigh of relief that she'd managed to arrive with everything, herself and Earl included, in one piece. "We made it, Earl," she said to the snoring cat as she dismounted and carefully leaned the bike against the back storeroom door.

Usually, Lilly would position her bike outside the front window and decorate it according to the season, hanging the tea of the day sign from the handlebars, but this evening her destination was the flat upstairs.

Lifting the heavy hamper from the basket, a voice called out, "Do you need some help, Lilly?" and she turned to see James Pepper, the father of her employee Stacey, approaching from the direction of the car-park.

"Hello, James. Yes, please. Could you take this hamper while I put my bike in the hallway?"

"Of course. I dropped off my contribution earlier, so I'm hands free as it were," he replied, taking the hamper from her and holding open the flat door while Lilly wheeled in her bike.

Earl chose that moment to stick his head out of Lilly's jumper and released an indignant meow. James jumped back in surprise.

"Good grief," he laughed. "What on earth are you wearing?"

Lilly gave a twirl. "It's great, isn't it? The latest thing for every respectable cat owner."

A Frosty Combination

"Mmm," James said. "Well, you're certainly a trend-setter if nothing else."

They climbed the stairs and knocked on the door, which was flung open a second later by an exuberant Stacey.

"Happy Thanksgiving!" she cried, giving them both hugs and pulling them inside.

The holiday was an American one and as such, Lilly had obviously never celebrated it before. According to Stacey, it was modelled on the harvest feast shared by the Pilgrims in 1621 and allows people to give thanks with friends and family for what they have. It's also a celebration of the Autumn, or fall as it's known in America, harvest.

"Happy Thanksgiving, Stacey," Lilly said, stepping inside.

STACEY HAD DECORATED the flat with streamers in autumnal colours, chubby pilgrims and paper turkeys, all of which were apparently commonly representative of the holiday.

"Stacey," Lilly said. "This looks fabulous. Where on earth did you get it all?"

"I made the streamers, but I asked mom if she'd send me the rest. You can't get pilgrims and paper turkey over here. I asked mom how to cook the turkey, too. It's in the oven. You two sure are early."

"You know, Stacey, the consensus is turkey wasn't actually served at the first thanksgiving," her father said, ever the university lecturer. "I believe the pilgrims mostly ate fish."

"Dad, if you want cod I can do it. But I'm having turkey," Stacey said, playfully punching his arm and laughing.

The bathroom door opened and Lilly saw that she and James weren't the only ones to have arrived early. Stacey's boyfriend, Frederick Warren, stepped out smiling.

"Hello, Mr Pepper," he said politely. "Hi, Lilly."

"Hello, Frederick," James said with a nod. As a mostly absent father until fairly recently, he was still getting used to being part of his daughter's life, so the whole boyfriend scenario was new to him. Although he and Fred had both worked alongside Stacey during Lilly's absences at the shop, they were still overly polite and slightly wary around one another. "So, how do you like working at the café?"

Fred beamed. "It's really good. Lilly and Abigail are both great to work for."

"He's picked it up really quickly, dad," Stacey said from the kitchen, where she was vigorously assaulting potatoes with a masher.

Fred nodded. "I'm looking forward to the grand re-opening. All the training Stacey has been giving us has kept me busy, but I want to put it into practice now. Hopefully I will remember everything."

Late summer and early autumn had been an exceptionally busy time for Lilly. Not only was she running her Tea Emporium, but she had invested in a local café with her former nemesis, Abigail Douglas. They'd closed it down to remodel, giving the place a fresh look and designed a brand new menu. They had hired new employees for the both the tea shop and the café with the idea that Lilly oversee her shop while Abigail ran the café. During that time, Stacey had been promoted to manager of both locations, which conversely allowed her more time for her university studies. She was responsible for training and scheduling the employee shifts at both premises, but was in charge of her own schedule. It was working well so far.

"You'll do great," Stacey assured Fred.

"Thanks," he replied with a grin. "Can I help with the potatoes?"

"Absolutely, this is killing my wrist," she said, sliding the bowl his way.

"Wow, look at all this food," Lilly exclaimed, adding her dishes to the plethora of goodies on the table, which she swore was groaning under the weight. "Is this really what a thanksgiving celebration looks like?"

"Yup!" Stacey said. "I hope you like it."

There was a knock at the door so Lilly went to answer it, as Stacey had put her father in charge of peeling sweet potatoes while she herself tackled a mountain of vegetables for yet another dish.

"Happy Turkey Day!" Archie called out when Lilly opened the door.

"Archie, how great to see you. Come in," she said, giving her friend and former co-worker a hug.

Archie was the senior investigative reporter with the local paper, The Plumpton Mallet Gazette, where Lilly had once been employed as the agony aunt. When the paper had been taken over by a larger concern, she was made redundant as they already had their own agony aunt on staff. It was Abigail Douglas, the woman she was now in partnership with. The irony was, now that Abigail had officially put in her notice with the paper, they were going to be without an agony aunt altogether.

"I hear Abigail is coming to this shindig," Archie said, unable to conceal the misgivings in his tone.

"Be nice to her, Archie. She's my business partner now."

"Better you than me, Lilly. I hope it all works out for you, though. I really do," Archie said, stepping past her to add his contribution to the table. "Golly, this food looks amazing."

"Thank you, Archie," Stacey said. "I've been cooking all day."

"She was cooking all day yesterday, too. Don't let her fool you," Fred said. "And preparing for three days before that."

As people started to trickle in, mostly Stacey's friends from college and a handful of teashop and café staff, Lilly mingled with the younger crowd, pleased to be able to spend some time with Stacey. The girl had recently returned from London having spent her first holiday with her father, so she hadn't seen her for a while. As soon as she'd returned to Plumpton Mallet, Stacey had dived into the staff training and university. This was the first time they'd really had a chance to chat and catch up with one another.

As the crowd grew louder and the noise levels rose, Lilly found herself on door duty to listen out for late arriving guests. There was a knock on the door and she opened it to find Abigail clutching a large chocolate orange trifle.

"Oh, that looks yummy, Abigail."

Abigail came in and her eyes fell towards Lilly's stomach. She raised a brow. "Are you wearing your cat?"

"I am," Lilly replied, turning so Earl could see Abigail. He meowed loudly, then pulled his head back inside the pocket, disappearing from sight. "He loves it. I've tried to let him out a few times, but he's perfectly content where he is."

"You really are ridiculous," Abigail said, laughing good naturedly.

"I know, but he deserves to be spoiled. He had a rough start in life. I don't think he likes all the noise, but Stacey said I can pop him into her room if it all gets too much for him. He spends a lot of his time there, anyway."

Abigail took a look at the vast crowd of people crammed into the small flat and nodded in agreement. "I don't blame him. If he does, I might just join him."

Lilly laughed. It was odd becoming friends and business partners with someone she had been at extreme loggerheads with in the not too distant past. Abigail had been, to put it mildly, difficult and obnoxious, going out of her way to cause Lilly problems. Now, however, she knew the real cause for her behaviour and she was seeing her in a new light altogether.

ABIGAIL SAID HELLO to everyone, handing over her trifle to Stacey while Lilly got her a drink. When she returned, they moved to a slightly quieter corner where they could sit and talk for a moment.

"Did you get everything settled with your solicitor, Abigail?"

Abigail nodded. "Up to a point. I'm afraid my ex-husband is coming after me for money."

Abigail's erratic attitude had induced Lilly to investigate the cause. Recently, Abigail had taken a holiday and left Plumpton Mallet with very little explanation. Eventually, Lilly had reached out to her and it turned out Abigail had come to Plumpton Mallet in order to flee an abusive ex-husband. Back in the early years of their marriage, Abigail's then husband had been a journalist. It was the reason she'd also got into the business. Eventually, he had become a professor, teaching journalism at various universities. However, due to his inability to work with others and his habit of flying of the handle at every perceived slight, warranted or not, he found himself without work more often than he was employed. With no job and no income, money had become a real problem, and he'd consequently lashed out as a result. It was Abigail who had been in the firing line.

"But surely he's got no claim on your money after all this time?" Lilly said now.

"That's what my solicitor says. He's an idiot to even try, but I suspect he's doing it to frighten me. Hopefully, things will settle down now I have legal representation. I'm just glad I'm taking my own path and doing something for me for a change."

After Lilly had approached her, she'd learned Abigail had always wanted to open her own business. A dream that had been crushed repeatedly by her ex due to his poor financial decisions and the control he had over her. With Lilly's favourite café recently coming onto the market and a healthy profit from her first trading year, Lilly had asked Abigail to go into partnership with her in a new venture. Abigail had been thrilled at the idea.

A Frosty Combination

"Well, try not to think about it too much," Lilly said. "It's just unnecessary stress. The trick now is to look ahead and keep busy. We've got a lot of marvelous things happening you can concentrate on."

"You're right. I am so excited to get the business up and running," Abigail said, sighing. "Lilly, I must say again how grateful I am for your support. After the way I behaved towards you, I still find it unbelievable that you would want to go into business with me."

Lilly shrugged. "Well, once you started talking to me instead of shouting, I was actually able to get to know the real you. It helped me understand what the cause was and the fact the person I thought you were wasn't the case at all. And you have had some excellent ideas for the café. Besides, I certainly couldn't have afforded it on my own. I'm looking forward to opening the doors."

"Do you think everything will be ready in time for the grand re-opening? After all the time and hard work we've put in, it is difficult to believe we actually open in just two days."

"Saturday is going to be very busy," Lilly said. "And probably a little crazy. But I think everyone is ready. Stacey has been working extremely hard training all the new staff."

"And then the Christmas Market is coming up too. I'm eager to get going with it, but it's a lot to deal with all at once. I feel like I've been thrown in at the deep end without a life belt."

"Oh, it's definitely sink or swim time, Abigail. But don't worry, you'll be fine and we'll have lots of support. Both James and Archie have volunteered to help with the market stalls."

"Archie?" Abigail questioned, looking over at the crowd around the table where Archie was chatting with some of Stacey's fellow students. "Do you really think he wants to work with me again?"

"He's only going to be helping with the initial setting up," Lilly said. "And he is a very good friend of mine, so I'd really like it if you two tried to get along."

"I stole from his desk," Abigail said, cringing in embarrassment.

It was true. In one of her less than impressive moments, Abigail had stolen evidence from Archie's desk in an attempt to give herself a leg up in her desire to become an investigative reporter. She had known she was fighting a losing battle being the town's agony aunt. Now, Lilly understood Abigail had been acting out of sheer desperation. If she lost her job, she'd be left with nothing, and the temptation to return home to the cycle of abuse she'd been trying to escape might have been too strong for her to resist.

"Yes, I know you did," Lilly said. "But remember, Abigail, you're not the same person now as you were then. Archie is willing to forgive and forget. You should talk to him, you know. It will help lay the ghosts to rest and enable you to move forward."

"Yes, I might just do that," Abigail said with a nervous smile, as Stacey called out that the Thanksgiving dinner was finally ready.

Chapter Two

*I*T WAS ALL hands on deck as the day to re-open the café finally arrived. With the exception of Stacey and one other employee who were both busy running the Tea Emporium, everyone Lilly and Abigail had hired was working hard to ensure every customer who walked through the café door was served quickly, efficiently and left satisfied. Making it more likely they would not only return, but recommend the place to others.

Since Lilly and Abigail had bought the café, it had undergone a complete makeover, both inside and out, to make it look like a sister business of the Tea Emporium. Although expensive, Lilly had opted for a durable medium oak hardwood floor, which set off the rest of the modern take on a vintage theme, which is what they'd both decided on. As with the tea shop, one of the walls had been taken back to the brickwork, then re-pointed and given several coats of matte varnish to make it hard wearing.

The individual tables were honey coloured wood, each with comfy bucket chairs upholstered in a chartreuse, cream and deep raspberry plaid, rather than the common spindle backs which Lilly found uncomfortable, especially on her spine, and a display of realistic dried flowers in tin milk jugs. These were currently a winter theme containing white roses, lavender blue thistles, Gypsophilia and eucalyptus foliage, but would be changed according to the season, holiday, or specifically tailored if they were running a particular event.

On the wall sides there were wooden booths with banquettes upholstered in soft, high-quality faux suede, with button backs imitating Chesterfields. The beauty of which was their stain resistant and water proof capabilities making it easy to wipe down if there were accidents. In a café, this was par for the course. The colour was a darker shade of chartreuse, a favourite of them both. They'd chosen various botanical print throw cushions to add to the comfort factor.

The final bits of the design were the individual chandeliers above the tables and booths, and several large faux potted ferns providing a garden feel as well as some privacy. Lilly had even sourced a couple of standard lamps with original tasseled shades and an old bookcase, which she filled with reading material and colouring books for those with children. The whole ambiance was that of an exclusive club and it was going down a storm with the patrons.

The young employees, mostly teens and college students, were darting about taking and serving orders and working hard in the kitchen. Fred was working as the barista, serving both coffees, much to Stacey's delight, and teas from Lilly's shop.

"We're running low on the new Chamomile blend," Fred told Lilly when she went to see how he was coping. He was filling teapots from the large vintage copper urn Abigail had found on an auction site and personally polished to such a shine, it looked brand new.

"Leave it with me, Fred, I'll get someone to bring over some boxes."

One of the new additions they had made was converting a small back storeroom into an office, which is where Lilly found Abigail a moment later counting cash.

"Golly, you look like Scrooge counting his wealth," Lilly said, laughing.

"I can't believe how many people have been through already. It's a triumph, Lilly. Most of them have paid with notes, so I need to get to the bank and replenish the till float or we'll run out of change. I'll be about ten minutes."

"No problem, you go ahead. I need to ring Stacey for more Chamomile, the staff are recommending it to go with the lunchtime special so it's going faster than I expected."

A quick call to Stacey and she said she'd send several boxes with Rodney Scott, one of the new staff members. He was only in his late twenties but knew almost as much about teas as she did. "Dad has just turned up anyway," Stacey continued. "And he's happy to help."

A few minutes later, Lilly went outside and spotted Rodney making his way down the street. In addition to the tea, he had an old camera hung round his neck. From what Lilly understood, he'd decided to return to college and was studying film and photography. Stacey had told her he was really good at it, having been to one of his exhibitions at the university.

Seeing the camera, Lilly suddenly remembered he'd offered to take some promotional photos of the open day.

"Hi, Rodney, thanks for bringing the tea," Lilly said, taking the boxes from him.

"You're welcome, Lilly," he said, holding up his camera. "I thought while I was here and had a break from the tea shop, I'd take some pictures of the open day. You have an amazing crowd here. I'm sure I'll get some good shots for the paper."

"That's great, Rodney, thank you. Go inside and take as many as you want."

"Would you mind if I did some creative shots as well? You can obviously use them for any promotions you have, but there's a possibility I could use a few in my next course exhibition."

"Of course, you can do whatever you like. It would be lovely to see some of our café images in your exhibition."

As Rodney moved between the tables taking photographs and chatting amiably with the patrons, Lilly went to unbox the teas and help Fred behind the counter. A couple of minutes later, Abigail returned with change, which she put in the till. Once they'd caught up with drink orders, Lilly positioned herself at the door in order to greet new customers. Two of whom she was especially pleased to see.

A Frosty Combination

"WELL, HELLO THERE," Lilly said, grinning at Bonnie and Archie. "I was hoping you two were going to show up today."

"You know we'll always be here to support you," Archie said. "Even if it means supporting Abigail as well."

"Archie Brown! Don't you be so mean."

"I know, I know," he said, giving her a peck on the cheek. "I was just having a little joke. She and I had a good talk at Stacey's thanksgiving celebration. We're fine now, don't worry. But I still need to give her a bit of stick from time to time. It's all part of the fun."

Bonnie rolled her eyes. "Are you sure this is a good time, Lilly? You look incredibly busy. Are there actually any seats left?"

"There's a couple in the far window I've been saving for you. Come in and I'll get you both a menu."

They walked through the tables, both Bonnie and Archie smiling and nodding at people they knew, until they reached their table. Lilly gave them a menu each and asked one of the waiting staff to look after them.

"Lilly," Archie said, before she disappeared. "I'm setting aside my crime reporting for a moment to write up a story on your grand re-opening. I'd like to get a couple of quotes from both you and Abigail if you have time?"

"Absolutely," Lilly said. "One of our staff members, Rodney, is taking pictures, too. If you want to have a word with him, he's already suggested some could be of use to the paper."

"I will do that. Thank you, Lilly. Now, off you pop while Bonnie and I see what scrumptious delights you have to offer us. I can see you're needed elsewhere."

Once again, Lilly found herself at the door greeting customers, but this time, she was joined by Abigail.

"Lilly, I'm absolutely stunned at how many customers we've had today, and still they come."

It was well past what would have been the usual lunch time rush, yet it didn't seem to be slowing down in the slightest. Clearly, the Plumpton Mallet townspeople had been eagerly waiting for the café to open again. The door opened and Lilly greeted the man who entered.

"Welcome, is it a table for one?"

"Monty!" Abigail gasped and suddenly grabbed Lilly's wrist.

"Abigail," the man said, scowling viciously. "I heard you'd bought a café and had to see it for myself. So this is what you did with the money you stole from me."

Lilly had heard the name Monty before and felt a surge of anger rise in her chest. This was Montgomery Douglas, Abigail's ex-husband. The abusive partner she'd fled from.

"I didn't steal anything from you, Monty," Abigail replied, and Lilly noticed the slight quiver in her voice. She was still clutching Lilly's wrist.

"Liar," he snarled. "You think I don't know what you've been doing? I've been keeping tabs on you ever since you walked out."

Lilly stood tall and manoeuvred herself in front of Abigail. She didn't want this to get out of hand. "This is neither the time nor the place, Mr. Douglas. If you're not here to eat, then I'd like you to leave."

A Frosty Combination

"Get lost," Monty said. "I'm here to talk to Abigail. It's none of your business. You can't hide from me forever, Abigail. You owe me a lot of money and I'm not going anywhere until you pay up."

"Leave me alone, Monty," Abigail said. "It was my money, not yours."

"You're a little snake and you're going to get what you deserve. I hope you know that?"

"How dare you threaten her?" Lilly hissed, glancing around to find several patrons watching the exchange with undisguised interest. Thankfully, things didn't get a chance to escalate as Bonnie joined them.

"Is everything all right over here?" she asked.

"Mind your own business," Monty said. "I'm trying to talk to my wife."

"Ex-wife," Abigail muttered, and Monty's eyes darted her way. Lilly felt Abigail flinch, which made her even more angry. She was sick at heart to find how much control her ex-husband still had over her. *Doesn't Monty live in London?* Lilly thought. *What is he doing here in Plumpton Mallet except purely to harass Abigail?*

"He's just leaving," Lilly said to Bonnie, but her eyes never left Monty.

"No, I don't think so," he said, pushing forward.

Bonnie's arm shot out to prevent him from taking one more step. With her free hand, she shoved her warrant card under his nose. "I suggest you leave quietly unless you want to see the inside of Plumpton Mallet's police station. From a cell."

He scoffed. "Keep your nose out of my business," he said, ignoring the warrant card completely. Lilly wondered if he'd even seen it, or if he really was just stupid? He pushed forward and this time Bonnie reacted with more force. Grabbing his outstretched arm, she wrenched it down, twisted it behind his back and frogmarched him out into the street before he realised what was happening. Abigail and Lilly close on her heels. "Now, you have a choice. You can stay, in which case I will formally arrest you. Or you can leave."

Behind them, some of the people in the café started to clap and one or two shouted out, 'Arrest him!' and 'Throw him in jail.' At the sound of the mocking, jeering crowd, Monty's face contorted in anger, but he seemed to realise he was in a precarious position.

"Fine! I'll go. But I'll be back, Abigail," he shouted over his shoulder. "Don't think you've heard the last of me."

As Monty wended his way across the market square, Abigail let out a shaky breath of relief.

"Are you okay?" Lilly asked.

"I didn't think he knew where I was," Abigail said, wringing her hands anxiously. "I moved here to get away from him."

"I'll make sure you have someone to see you home tonight, Abigail. You're not going alone."

"Really? Oh, thank you, Bonnie."

"That was an excellent move, Bonnie," Lilly said. "I don't think he knew what hit him until he was in the street."

Rodney walked over from where he'd been standing watching the proceedings, eyes on stalks. "What was that all about?" he asked.

"That was my ex-husband," Abigail said, shaking her head. "He's a nasty piece of work."

"I can tell," Rodney said, and lifted his camera. "However, I'm quite sure I managed to get an excellent picture of him being marched outside like a criminal by one of our police forces' finest. I could develop one for you if you like?" he said with a grin.

Lilly and Abigail both laughed, but Abigail declined a copy of the photo. "Thank you, Rodney, but I don't want to see his face ever again."

"Well I'll have one," Bonnie said. "That was one of best moves recently. I'll hang it in the station as a warning."

Chapter Three

THE GRAND RE-OPENING of the café had been a resounding success and had surpassed, by a country mile, the expectations of both Lilly and Abigail, as well as Stacey and all the other staff. As the days continued, the café was full constantly, partly due to the superb article Archie had put together for the paper, complemented by three of Rodney's photographs, and word of mouth. It seemed everyone who had visited so far had recommended it to their family and friends. Lilly knew without a doubt they had a winner on their hands. All the little kinks in the processes had been ironed out, and now everything was running like clockwork, it was time to turn their attention to their next event, the annual Christmas Market.

Lilly, Abigail and Stacey were in the back room of the Tea Emporium with notebooks full of to-do lists, ideas and plans. Stacey also had her laptop out and was transferring the actions to a spreadsheet.

"We've still got quite a lot to do if we're going to be ready for market day," Abigail said.

She was very good at taking charge and had turned out to be an efficient event planner. Since Lilly and Stacey had been dipping their toes into this arena for a while, with more of an ad hoc approach, it was a relief to have someone on board who really knew how to plan, organise and run these types of functions.

"I know," Lilly said. "It's staggering how much we still have outstanding. Let's start with some of the general items and add in the details. Stacey, how's the cross-training going?"

Stacey had been hard at work training the staff so they could all work efficiently at both the café and the tea shop. While some would obviously have a preferred location, this would create the opportunity to find last-minute replacements for either site, or allow them to work on extra event days.

"Fred and Jean are ready to go wherever you put them. Rodney struggles a bit on the barista station, but that's to be expected. We have quite a complicated coffee menu for someone more used to serving teas. But he's mastered pretty much every other position in the café. I'm conscious of the fact we might be spreading some people too thin, and I think Rodney would do better training in the kitchen. Besides, we have a lot of capable baristas already."

"Yes, that's a good point," Abigail said, making notes as Stacey talked.

"So, this is what I've been working on," Stacey said, turning her computer so the others could see the detailed spreadsheet on the screen. "Basically under each employee's name, it shows the areas they've been trained and approved to work on, stock room, teashop, register, café service, barista station, etc. Using a star system. Don't worry, I'll have all this available in the scheduling app I've implemented."

"Stacey, this is excellent work, well done," Lilly said. "But an app? This is the first I've heard of an app."

"It's super easy to use," Stacey said, whipping out her phone. "I found this free app that the staff have all downloaded now. It keeps track of everyone's schedules and I can change anything from my phone. They get an alert to their phone when they have a shift to do and in what position. I do it every two weeks. If I needed to cover a particular shift because that person is out sick or something, I click on that shift and it will give me a list of people available who can work at that position."

"That's amazing, Stacey," Abigail said. "And you've made profiles for me and Lilly?"

"Yeah. Here, let me have your phones and I'll download the app and get your accounts set up."

Once that was done and the two of them had been briefed on the basics, Lilly asked about where each staff member would be on the Christmas Market day. "Do you think Rodney could manage to run the tea stall himself that day?"

Stacey nodded. "I think so. We're only offering a few teas on the day. It's mostly just merchandise for sale, like tea-sets and teapots and boxes of tea. We're doing a special offer discount coupon from the stand so people can come into the shop proper for samples, and me and dad will be running the shop that day. Archie also said he'd run the stall if and when Rodney needs a break or another set of hands when it's busy."

"I'll be doing the café's stand," Abigail said. "And I spoke to the market organiser at the council and she's moving our stands next to one another like we asked. That way we can help each other if need be. And Bonnie has also volunteered to be my assistant for the day should things be too busy for one person."

"That's all very well planned, Abigail," Lilly said. "So who do we have running the café?"

"Everyone else, with Fred in charge," Stacey said. "And Jean is head server, so it should all run efficiently."

"Well, it looks as though everything really is on schedule as far as staffing is concerned. As for me, I'll be bouncing from place to place as needed. So, any more questions?"

Stacey looked pensively at Abigail. "I do have one," she said, and Lilly immediately guessed what it was about.

❦

*L*ILLY NODDED FOR her to speak what was on her mind.

"It's about what happened at the café. I know you probably want to forget about it, but do you think your ex-husband is still in Plumpton Mallet, Abigail?"

"Unfortunately, I think he is, yes. Are you worried he'll turn up at the market?"

Stacey nodded. "A little. I'm relieved Bonnie will be with you, though. Maybe he'll behave himself?"

"Actually, I think that's why Bonnie volunteered to help me. I believe he'll have second thoughts about causing any trouble if she's around. I hope so anyway. I don't think I could stand another confrontation."

Rodney chose that moment to pop his head round the storeroom door to see if it was okay to grab some more samples to stock up the cabinet. Lilly said, of course it was.

"Oh, by the way," he said. "I developed that photograph last night if you want to see it?"

"Absolutely," Stacey said, holding out her hand. Rodney took the photo from his satchel in the staff area and handed it to her. Stacey burst out laughing. "Look at his face. Wow, you really caught the shock and indignation. And how cool does Bonnie look? She'll love this in her office."

Lilly and Abigail also had a look, Abigail blushing to the tip of her ears, but she, too, laughed.

"You have no idea how much I appreciate having you all supporting me," Abigail said, handing the photo back to Rodney. "Ever since I first came to Plumpton Mallet, I've been awful to everyone. I just felt so alone, isolated, and had got used to being hostile all the time to save me from being hurt. My trust in everyone had completely gone, and I was constantly in flight or fight mode. You don't know how wonderful it is to have a community and allies around me. Thank you."

Lilly smiled. "You're among friends now, Abigail. We'll always be here for you," she said, quickly reaching across and squeezing Abigail's arm in support. "Now, Rodney, would you mind brewing some of my new tea for us all to try? It's the holiday blend I've done, especially for the Christmas market. I'd like to know what you all think?"

"Of course. I'll do it now," Rodney said, returning to the shop.

Several minutes later, having first taken time to re-stock the shelves, he was back with a tray containing a full teapot and four cups. He poured one for each of them and they took a tentative sip. It was a peppermint and cranberry blend, and as each of them sampled the brew, they unanimously agreed it was going to be a huge hit.

"This is amazing," Rodney said. "I think this will be very popular."

"I agree," Stacey said, and Abigail nodded. "This might be my new favourite," she said. "Did you do this blend yourself?"

"I did," Lilly said, feeling quite proud of her new creation.

After that, Abigail also brewed up samples of her peppermint orange cocoa, which she intended to sell on both the café stand, and in the café itself over the holiday period. For this, she got a round of applause from the others.

"This is amazing, Abigail," Stacey said. "You should have the option of mini marshmallows as a topping."

"Oh, that's a very good idea, Stacey," Abigail said, making a note.

"So, do you want to see what I've been working on?" Stacey said.

"What? You mean you've done even more than the scheduling and the app?" Lilly asked.

"Yeah, I actually dabble a bit in digital design. It's kind of a hobby." She found a document on her laptop and turned it so they could view. "I've already found an excellent deal for the printing of holiday 'takeout' cups, so if you like the design I can order and they will deliver in time for the market."

The design was beautiful. Blue cups covered in snowflakes with different text on both sides. The first read *The Tea Emporium,* with the address and the second *The Agony Aunt's Café,* again with the address.

"What a brilliant name!" exclaimed Lilly and Abigail at once. "I know we've been wracking our brains for something suitable, but I can't believe we didn't think of this," Abigail said. "It's perfect."

When Lilly had first spoken to the council officials, they had approved The Tea Emporium name immediately, so she was sure they would do the same for The Agony Aunt's café. The name would tie in both partners and link it with the tea shop. It was perfect branding. Lilly made a note to call her contact at the council immediately to get the ball rolling. Hopefully it would be all be confirmed before the Christmas Market day.

"It's brilliant, Stacey, and if Abigail agrees, I'd say order the cups now and I'll get on to the council about the official café signage."

Abigail nodded. "I agree wholeheartedly. The name and the design are exactly what we need. Well done, Stacey."

"So, is that everything on the list?"

"Just one other thing," Stacey said. "The Secret Santa. You two need to draw first." She reached over to the kitchen shelf and retrieved a chipped teapot. "I've included everyone; the seasonal staff and our volunteers, as well as the proper employees. So, Dad, Bonnie and Archie are in there too."

Lilly and Abigail took turns drawing out a slip of paper.

"Remember, don't tell anyone who you got. We'll be doing the big reveal at the staff Christmas Party later."

"Right, if there's nothing else I need to get back to the café," Abigail said, tucking the name she'd drawn from the teapot in her pocket.

"See you later, Abigail," Lilly said.

Stacey stretched, arms raised above her head, and let out a groan. "I'm going to order these cups now then go on my break."

"Thank you, Stacey," Lilly said.

Once she'd left, Lilly unfurled the piece of paper she'd drawn and looked at the name. She frowned. She had drawn Stacey's father, James. "Now, what on earth am I to get you for Christmas?" she said.

Chapter Four

THE DAY OF the Plumpton Mallet Christmas Market had finally arrived and Lilly arose early, full of excitement and a little trepidation. The setting up of all the vendor's stalls with their sturdy red and green striped canvas roofs had taken place the day before courtesy of the town council and their army of workers, now all that was needed was to stock the shelves and set out the displays. As Lilly approached, she could see it was all well underway at The Agony Aunt's café and The Tea Emporium booths.

The council had also done a fantastic job with decorating the square this year, with a plethora of multi-coloured fairy lights strung across its entire width. It was like walking beneath a canopy of stars. Lights also hung around each stall, along with faux snow and a huge fully dressed Christmas tree took pride of place in the centre.

A Frosty Combination

At one side of the square was a Santa's Grotto for the children, and at the other a Nativity scene with live animals from the local rescue sanctuary. It was a small fee to enter and pet or feed the little lambs, the two donkeys and the two calves, all of them already happily munching on their assorted breakfasts and being looked after by the manager of the rescue. The money went towards the upkeep of the sanctuary and there were several parents with excited children already milling about, waiting for it to open.

As Lilly's job was to keep an eye on all the separate locations, lending a hand when needed and being the runner for re-stocking when necessary, she chose to go to the tea shop first, where Earl was safe from the hustle and bustle in the flat above, and Stacey and James were already hard at work. James, thanks to his daughter, had become well versed in the art of tea and was proving to be an excellent support to Stacey. Already, he was showing Lilly's latest stock of Christmas themed tea sets to a handful of patrons who had obviously waiting outside for the shop to open.

"Stacey gave me a crash course," he said after he'd sold two of the new sets, one a white bone china with gold rims and a beautiful illustration of a snowman and his family on the front, the other consisting of a Christmas village, with the teapot shaped as the church, the sugar bowl as a little shop with the roof as the lid, and the milk jug like a dairy. He watched with an indulgent smile on his face as the happy customers left, clutching their purchases.

"I really do appreciate you helping, James," Lilly said. "So, are you looking forward to the holiday?"

"I am. Christmas is my favourite time of the year, but this year will be extra special because I will have Stacey with me. It's our first Christmas together since she was small."

Lilly smiled. James had certainly come a long way since she'd first met him. "Will you be spending it in London or here in Plumpton Mallet?"

"We'll have most of the month here, in town, but Christmas week we'll be in London. The city is truly spectacular at this time of year and I very much want her to see it. She's already got cover for her shifts organised and college term will be over, so it's all looking very promising. We didn't have many Christmas traditions when I was growing up, I'm hoping to start some new ones together."

"That's such a lovely idea, James," Lilly said, wondering if there was something she could get for his secret Santa that the two of them could do together. She spent a couple more minutes chatting and double checking the two of them were all right, then headed down to the café.

The market was already flooded with people and Lilly could hear Christmas carols being sung by the school choirs. The Plumpton Mallet Gazette had three of their staff dressed up in Dickensian outfits handing out free copies of the special market edition, full of advertisers touting their wares. All the shop windows surrounding the square were heavily decorated, Christmas themes being the favourite of many of them. And as Lilly looked up at the lights, a snowflake landed on her cheek. *Just perfect*, she thought happily, as the flakes began to fall properly. It really added to the ambiance and made it magical.

A Frosty Combination

The café was exceptionally busy when Lilly arrived, with people waiting for a table while chatting happily outside. Inside, Fred was efficiently running the place and Lilly observed for a while before she walked over.

"How are things going, Fred?"

"Totally brilliant. The atmosphere is great, especially with the Christmas songs we're playing. It's like Santa's grotto in here. And everyone wants one of the take away mugs Stacey designed. We've actually got a waiting list for them," he said, waving a notebook.

"Wow, really? That's excellent news. I think I'll get her to design some for other holidays as well. Perhaps they can become collector's items?"

"Hey, that's a great idea. And Abigail's cocoa is really popular. People are coming here after trying it at the stall. And, well, I hope you don't mind, but I tried something special myself."

"You did? What is it?"

"Come over to the barista counter," he said, and she followed to where Jean was serving a queue of customers wanting hot beverages to take away with them. Fred waited until she'd finished. "Jean, could you make Lilly one of the peppermint cocoa mochas we've been selling?"

"I can," she said, and a minute later Lilly was sipping Fred's newly invented coffee.

"Fred," Lilly said, her eyes lighting up. "This is one of the best coffees I've ever tasted. Well done. Could you do another one for Abigail and I'll take it over to her?"

She assured Fred he was doing a superb job, thanked Jean for making the coffee, then headed back outside. In the band stand there was a brass band playing Christmas tunes, and in a large marquee at the back she could see other performers getting ready. There would be live music playing all day and well into the evening.

Everywhere she looked, there were people drinking from the distinctive blue cups with their snowflake design, and she grinned. The teas, coffees and cocoa were obviously very popular and what fantastic free advertising. Stacey had done an amazing job. As she approached the café stand, she could see Abigail and Bonnie hanging up shirts with the new logo on the front.

"Hi, you two. Those shirts look great. I never got the chance to see them."

Plumpton Mallet council had immediately approved the name and The Agony Aunt's Café was now official. The signage for the café itself was still being made. However, they'd managed to get collapsible signs for the booth and Stacey had ordered some tee shirts and sweatshirts as well. The logo was a teacup shaped ink well with a quill and was printed in the middle of the shirt along with the café name.

"Do we have enough for the staff to change into today?" Lilly asked. "The warmer ones, considering it's snowing."

"We have plenty," Abigail said. "Isn't the snow wonderful? We couldn't have asked for more perfect timing."

"And I'm wearing one of the sweatshirts," Rodney said from the stall next door. He came out and gave an exaggerated twirl. "I thought it would help people understand the concept that the café and the tea shop are part of the same brand."

"It suits you, Rodney, and good thinking. Have you finished setting up or do you need me to help?"

A Frosty Combination

"I've finished, however, Archie seems to think whatever I put out needs re-doing, so I've left him to it."

"Presentation is everything," Archie said, slipping to the front of the stall, casting a discerning eye over the whole display, then moving a teaspoon a centimetre to the left. She noticed he was wearing a forest green waistcoat with a holly berry design. It suited him.

Lilly laughed, then remembered Abigail's coffee. "Here, try this. Fred made up this coffee recipe."

Abigail took a sip, her eyes widening. "My, that's very good. I'll remember to congratulate him when I see him later."

"Do you fancy walking around the other stalls with me, Lilly?" Bonnie asked. "I doubt we'll have time later when the coaches arrive and everything gets even busier."

"Good idea. Abigail, would you be okay if I did that?"

"Of course, you go ahead. I'll have a look later and you can fill in for me then."

With that arranged, Lilly and Bonnie started a meandering stroll around the square and the many vendor booths.

THERE WAS ROW upon row of market stalls, all selling an incredible array of stunning items, and both Lilly and Bonnie were enthralled. One vendor had a range of handmade traditional wooden toys and Christmas tree ornaments, beautifully carved and painted in extraordinary detail. Steam trains with moving parts that ran on tiny tracks. Tiny rocking horses that actually rocked. Teddy bears with moving limbs and drummer boys drumming. Nutcracker soldiers in their red and blue uniforms with mouths that opened, and fairies with fluttering gossamer wings. Lilly was very taken with a full set of ornaments based on the carol The Twelve Days of Christmas, particularly the detailing of Three French Hens. It came in a large shelved display shaped like a Christmas tree and would look perfect in her cottage. She made a mental note to come back when she had more time.

Another vendor was selling artisan gin with a range of complementary botanicals to put in the bottom of the glass. Lilly bought a bottle each of the Apple and hibiscus and the Pear and Blackberry. They'd make fabulous cocktails. While Bonnie opted for a Yorkshire Marmalade one and an Elderflower, Chamomile and Lemon Verbena blend.

Next door was a silversmith showing a stunning selection of unusual jewellery and they spent several happy minutes perusing the whole selection.

The Plumpton Mallet Christmas market was always a well advertised and well patronised affair, attracting people from all over the country as well as all the residents. It injected a much needed source of revenue into not just the town, but the local craftspeople and the businesses. This year, however, it was a much bigger event than any previous one Lilly could remember. Lilly smiled as a cute little girl with a shock of blonde curls beneath a red bobble hat, probably no more than five years old, tottered past gripping her mother's hand tightly and asked if this was the North Pole where Santa lived? Her bright blue eyes, as big as saucers, were shining in excitement.

A Frosty Combination

She and Bonnie stopped at a stall displaying exquisite blown glass ornaments and were immediately transfixed by the large Christmas tree covered in glass ornaments.

"These are incredible," Lilly said, gently holding a bauble shaped like a tree with tiny hanging ornaments. "It must have taken ages to get this so perfect."

"Look at this," Bonnie said, astounded. It was a perfect miniature working carousel, all in different coloured glass, with zebras, ostriches, tigers, and hippos instead of the more usual horses.

"That's breathtaking," Lilly said.

"And here's one with different breeds of dogs," Bonnie said. "Oh, I really love this one. Look at the Staffy and the Bull Terrier. They're so lifelike. I can't believe they are made of glass."

"If you want to see different colours, designs, or sizes, I've probably got them," a young woman said, popping up from behind the table where she was adding delicate glass figurines to a display.

"Laura Smith, I should have known this fabulous work was yours," Lilly said happily. "I remember your stall from last year, but I don't remember you having so much as you do today."

"Hello, Lilly. It's good to see you again. Business has been great since I was here last. I completely sold out last year, but too early unfortunately. I could have sold everything twice over, so I wanted to be fully prepared this year. I've invested a huge amount to make sure I've got enough for today."

"I'm sure it will be a huge success, Laura, it's stunning work."

It took Lilly and Bonnie quite a while to look through what Laura had put out for sale so far. There were rows upon rows of small glass animals, ballet dancers, a family set of gold nutcrackers, and an unusual set of Russian nesting dolls that Lilly thought was amazing. There was also a huge selection of large round baubles in a striking rainbow of colours. Lilly wondered if she could find something suitable for James among them all.

"I've a few more boxes to unpack," Laura said. "So if you're looking for something in particular I can keep it mind."

"I'll come back, Laura, when you've got everything set up. There's a number of things I would love."

"Me too," Bonnie said, eyeing the dog carousel again with undisguised interest.

Three quarters of an hour later, back at the tea and café stalls, they found Abigail adding some finishing touches to the displays in the form of seasonal greenery and red ribbons, while Rodney took photos.

"Oh, does that say hot cocoa?" a man's voiced boomed from behind.

"It does. I've just made the first batch if you'd like some?" Abigail said, turning to face her latest customer.

"Please. Peppermint orange cocoa will put me in the holiday spirit," he said. Glancing from the café to the tea booth. "Agony Aunts? So which one of you is an Agony Aunt?" he said, blushing slightly while he took out his wallet.

Lilly and Abigail both lifted their hands. "That would be both of us," Lilly said.

Bonnie did the monetary exchange while Abigail poured the drink.

A Frosty Combination

"You look familiar," the man said as Abigail handed him his mug.

"I was going to say the same about you," she replied hesitantly.

"Tom Livingstone."

Abigail's face fell. "Oh," she said. Then, aware she sounded rude, changed her tone. "It's, um, nice to see you again. Abigail. Abigail Douglas."

"Oh."

"Tom Livingstone," Bonnie said. "Have you just put in a job application at the police station?"

The man looked mortified for some reason and his eyes ranged from Bonnie to Abigail, then back again. "Are you DS Phillips?"

Bonnie nodded. "That's right. I believe we have an interview scheduled for later this week."

While Bonnie, Abigail and Tom were chatting, Lilly moved to the tea shop stall and helped Rodney prepare several mugs of the holiday tea for the queuing customers, but she had one ear open and was listening to the adjacent conversation. She noticed how uncomfortable Tom and Abigail appeared with one another.

"You've noticed how weird that whole exchange is next door, too?" Rodney whispered at her side.

Lilly nodded, but said nothing. Once she and Rodney had finished serving, she went back to the café stall and found Tom Livingstone had left.

"Are you all right, Abigail? What was that all about?"

"He's from London," Bonnie answered. "He's put in for a job at the station, but I'm not sure about him. He lost his last job for some reason. I planned to ask why at his interview."

"Don't give him a job, Bonnie," Abigail said, almost pleading.

Bonnie looked at her curiously. "Why? What is it, Abigail?"

"I know why he lost his job. He was best friends with my ex-husband. The one and only time I plucked up enough courage to contact the police because of Monty's abuse, it was Tom who turned up. He convinced me to let it go and not press charges. I found out it wasn't the first time he'd got my ex-husband out of trouble, either. Eventually he did it one too many times and covered up something serious for Monty and he got found out. I don't know what it was, but that's when he lost his job."

Bonnie squeezed Abigail's arm. "Thank you for telling me. He's definitely not the sort of person we want working at the station. It's no wonder he looked so ill when he realised who you were. He knew you'd share that tidbit with me the second he walked away."

"Yes," Abigail said. "I'd say so. Anyway, would you mind if I took a break to look around the stalls now?"

"No, of course not," Lilly said. "You go ahead. But why not take Bonnie with you just to be on the safe side? I don't want you bumping into your ex-husband or one of his cronies on your own."

Abigail smiled. "Do you want to do a little more shopping, Bonnie?"

"Yes I do. I almost bought something from Laura Smith earlier. I'd like to go back now she's finished unpacking, to see what else she has before I commit to buying it."

A Frosty Combination

"Well then, let's go before it's all gone. The crowd is getting bigger now."

Lilly smiled, watching Abigail and Bonnie walk away, talking animatedly. It wasn't too long ago that they couldn't stand the sight of one another. *How things change*, she thought.

She was busy non-stop over the hour they were away, as was Rodney at the tea stall, and was thrilled to note how popular the Agony Aunt's apparel was. She was well on her way to selling out and by the time her friends returned, she was down to the last half dozen.

"Crikey, you two look as though you enjoyed yourselves," she said, as Abigail and Bonnie returned laden with shopping bags and parcels.

"Oh, Lilly, you won't believe how many talented people there are here. There's an artisan cheese shop that is amazing. I've stocked up on quite a bit. And I've bought some fantastic gin. Oh, and did you manage to see the wooden toy stall? It reminds me of the handmade toys we had as children. And there's one stall with beautiful African carvings. Oh, and did you manage to go to the silversmith?"

Lilly had to laugh as Abigail prattled on about all the incredible things she'd seen. It was her first experience of the Plumpton Mallet Christmas market and she was certainly making up for lost time. She had never sounded so animated and happy.

Then a voice next door spoiled it all.

"I THOUGHT I TOLD you you're not welcome here," Rodney spat, clenching his fists.

Lilly looked up to see Monty Douglas almost at the tea stall, a smug look on his face. She dashed over.

"Is everything all right, Rodney?"

"He came earlier, when you and Bonnie were shopping. Archie and I told him to leave, but it looks like he can't stay away."

"Where was Abigail at the time?" she whispered.

"Hiding from him," he whispered back.

"You can't tell me where I can and can't go," Monty snarled. "It's a free country."

"Look," Lilly said. "I don't want any trouble. Please leave. Bonnie's here and I'm sure she'd be quite happy to escort you out of town."

Monty's cheeks flushed slightly. "I'm not here to start any trouble."

"Then what do you want, Monty?" Abigail said, stepping into view.

"I just want to talk, Abbie," he said, holding up his hands. "That's all."

"After what happened at the café, Monty, I find that very hard to believe. I don't think you're even capable of having a civil conversation."

Monty exhaled long and hard. He put his hands in his pockets, plainly resisting the urge to use them, and looked away for a second. "I just wanted to apologise for the other day."

Abigail's mouth fell open. Lilly had to bite her tongue, because she didn't buy this sudden change of heart for a second. Thankfully, neither did Abigail.

"If you have something to say, then you can say it here in front of my friends. I have no intention of being alone with you, Monty. I don't trust you."

"Fine," he huffed. "It's like I said. I just want to say sorry for how I acted at your café. I suppose it took me being thrown out by that chit of a policewoman to see sense."

Abigail nodded. "You've been out of line plenty of times before, Monty, and I suppose I should accept your apology. However, you're no longer my problem. You can go now, you've said your piece. I don't want anything to do with you ever again."

Suddenly, his Mr Nice guy act was gone. "You know what? I don't have to listen to your smart mouth anymore, either. We need to talk about that money you stole from me."

"For the last time, Monty, I did not steal that money. It was mine. I left your share in the bank. Now, just let it go and leave me alone."

"No, I don't think I will," he said, stepping closer.

Lilly and Rodney immediately stepped into his path, blocking him from reaching his ex-wife. Bonnie had also positioned herself close by, ready to pounce if things got out of hand. Lilly glanced down to see Monty's hands balled into fists. He was obviously spoiling for a fight, but before he made any attempt, Tom Livingstone appeared and rested a firm hand on his shoulder.

"Long time no see, Monty," he said in a friendly but stern timbre. "Let's calm down before this escalates, shall we?"

Monty was obviously surprised to see his old mate Tom in the middle of the small town. "What the blazes are you doing here?" he asked in a foul tone.

"I've come for the Christmas market," Tom replied casually. "What about you? You've not come all this way just to harass your ex-wife, have you? What do you say about letting sleeping dogs lie, eh? Go now, before you do something you'll regret."

Monty jerked his shoulder from under Tom's hand. "Since when do you care what goes on between me and my wife?"

"I believe Abigail is your ex-wife now, Monty. Leave her alone."

"Wind your neck in, Livingstone," Monty snapped.

Tom rolled his eyes. "As civil as ever, aren't you? Well, I'm not helping you out of this mess, Monty. Not after you lost me my job."

"I don't need your help," Monty snarled, his entire body stiffening as his anger rose. "I'm just here for the money that tramp stole from me."

"For the last time, it wasn't your money, Monty!" Abigail said in frustration.

"Shut up, woman," Monty said without looking at her. Instead, he was glaring at Tom with an increasing amount of hatred. "And you," he said to Tom, stabbing a finger in his chest. "You're not fooling anyone," he glanced quickly at Bonnie and a knowing, vicious smile appeared on his red face. "Oh, now I get it. You're here to see if you can get a job with the local plod. Well, I doubt they'll be stupid enough to take you, Livingstone. Not as corrupt as you are. I'm right, aren't I? You don't want to make a bad first impression with one of the local Bobbies?"

"Detective," Bonnie said. "And I think you should both leave now before I arrest the pair of you for..."

A Frosty Combination

Bonnie was unable to finish her sentence before Monty abruptly shoved Tom in the chest, causing him to stumble back. "You want to show off? Go ahead, do something," he jeered, egging him on.

Tom didn't hesitate. He swung a fist, landing a solid punch against Monty's jaw. Monty immediately retaliated, clipping Tom's temple and sending him staggering sideways into an oncoming pushchair. Bonnie pushed past to intercede. Standing between them with a forceful hand on each of their chests, she pushed them apart. She was not going to put up with a brawl in the middle of the market. Rodney grabbed Monty roughly by the arms and put him in a tight choke hold, twisting an arm behind his back so forcefully Monty yelled out, while Lilly and Abigail restrained Tom.

"You've both had enough warnings," Bonnie shouted. "You have two minutes to leave or I will throw you both in a cell. Together. Then I'll gladly sit back and watch you punch one another's lights out. But you will not fight here, understood? And, Monty, if you ever come near Abigail again you will be arrested and charged." She looked at each of the men one at a time. "Do I make myself clear?"

Tom nodded, Monty just scoffed, but they left in opposite directions. *Crisis averted for now*, Lilly thought. But wondered how long it would last.

AS SOON AS the two men were out of sight, the others congratulated Bonnie on diffusing the situation without any damage. A small crowd had formed around both of the stalls. *People by nature love drama*, Lilly thought, but it was good for business as everyone bought something.

Archie arrived back, arms loaded with more shopping bags than both Bonnie and Abigail combined.

"I saw that," he said. "What on earth happened while I was gone? Honestly, I can't leave you alone for five minutes."

"Actually, you've been gone for over an hour," Rodney said, grinning. "Why don't you put the bags in your car before you rejoin me?"

"I've finished my Christmas shopping," Archie said. "All done and dusted in an hour. That's the way to do it. And Bonnie, I have no idea what happened here, but well done. I'm sure they deserved it."

"We'll give you the inside info when you get back, Archie," Abigail said. "Bonnie was fabulous."

Archie wandered away to his car and Lilly asked if the others would mind if she nipped back to Laura's booth? "I want to get one of her ornaments before she sells it."

"No problem," Rodney said. "I can handle the stall until you get back." Abigail gave her a thumbs up in agreement, while she dealt with a new customer.

On her way to the glass stall, Lilly browsed through some of the other vendor's offerings. Those who hadn't been set up when she and Bonnie had come past earlier. She was hoping to find inspiration for her gift for James, as so far she was drawing a blank. She didn't really know him well enough to make an informed decision.

She had almost arrived at Laura's booth and could see the beautiful array of glass shining in the light, making rainbow prisms of colour. It was quite magical and certainly very festive. A moment later, she spied Monty coming in the opposite direction, hands in his pockets and a scowl on his face. As he was a bully by nature, particularly where women were concerned, she imagined it rankled a lot that he'd been bested by a female and his ego was badly bruised. She couldn't say she was sorry.

Just as Monty was level with Laura's booth, something totally unexpected happened. Tom appeared out of nowhere. He launched himself across the avenue of vendors and catapulted himself right into Monty. Monty was taken by complete surprise, and barely had time to take his hands out of his pockets to defend himself before they both flew back, crashing into Laura's beautiful glass display.

The sounds of shattering glass was like a lead weight in Lilly's stomach. "Oh, no!" she said, rushing to the scene.

She found Laura in a state of shock, tears pooling in her eyes as she tried to take in the scene of devastation before her. All her hard work and investment over the last year had been utterly ruined, and still the two men responsible were tussling on the ground.

"You idiots!" Lilly shouted, surprising herself at the volume of her own voice. "Have you any idea how much effort went into the creation of these products? And now you've ruined it all. You're supposed to be grown men, but you're acting like children! You should be ashamed of yourselves."

Her shouting had caused not only Bonnie, but another officer who'd been patrolling the market at the other end, to come charging to the area. Bonnie's eyes widened when she arrived, then it quickly turned to anger.

While Lilly would have liked Monty handcuffed and dragged away, she, and everyone else who had borne witness to the fight, knew it was Tom Livingstone who'd been the instigator. He was grabbed by Bonnie and handed over to her colleague. As the constable took him away, she turned her attention to Monty Douglas. He had what appeared at first glance to be a serious cut on his head from the glass, and Bonnie initially suggested the hospital as it looked like it might need stitches. However, as Monty used a handkerchief to apply pressure, the bleeding stopped, and there didn't appear to be any glass in the wound. He snapped at Bonnie, telling her he was fine.

"I want you to leave Plumpton Mallet immediately. You are now officially banned from ever entering this town again. Do you understand?"

"Yeah, I get it!"

With her arm around Laura in comfort, Lilly glanced back to find Abigail and Rodney hurrying over.

Bonnie looked pointedly at Monty. "Why are you still here? If you don't require an ambulance, then leave. Now."

"I'm leaving," he hissed at her. "I'm finished with this stupid place. But I'm not finished with you, woman," he said, glaring at his ex-wife with a murderous look.

And with those final words, Monty stormed off through the falling snow. Abigail looked at Laura's ruined stall and gasped, horrified.

"Oh, please don't tell me Monty did that?"

"Not exactly," Lilly said. "Tom came out of nowhere and rugby tackled him into the display. I'll stay back and help

Laura tidy up. See if we can salvage anything. Can you cope with running both stalls without me?"

"Of course," Abigail said at once. "Archie is back now as well. He's on his own at the moment, so we better get back, actually. Between the three of us, we'll manage, don't worry. You help poor Laura."

Bonnie said she'd also go back with Abigail and Rodney to lend a hand, so Lilly and Laura began to clear up the mess along with a council volunteer. They always came out in force during town events to ensure Plumpton Mallet stayed tidy. He was armed with sweeping brushes, dustpans, and a large bucket. But first he cordoned off the area to prevent anyone, including the numerous dogs who were walking around the market with their owners, from getting hurt.

Several of the other vendors, shocked and saddened at what had happened to Laura's beautiful inventory, also came forward to help, murmuring commiserations.

Anywhere there were larger pieces of glass, Laura sifted through to see if anything could be saved and repaired. Sadly, there was very little that could be fixed. As she worked, Lilly spotted among the debris on the table the little grey cat she'd been coming originally to purchase, and picked it up. One of the ears had snapped in half, but this made Lilly grin. She took it over to Laura.

"I'd like to buy this, Laura."

"But it's broken."

"I know, but so is my cat. I already thought it resembled him, but now it couldn't be more perfect. Earl Grey has part of his ear missing, too. Courtesy of street fight when he was a stray, probably. Do you think you could touch up around the sharp bit so I don't cut myself?"

"Yes, of course I can, but, Lilly, you aren't buying a broken ornament because you feel sorry for me, are you?"

"Absolutely not. I was going to buy it anyway and now, for me at least, it's better than it was originally. I'm so sorry this had to happen to you, Laura. I know how much money and time you've invested. I'm really heartbroken for you."

"Me too. It takes hours just to make one of these little animals. But on the bright side, I am insured. It just means I don't have much to sell again this year. But now we've tidied up, I'll display what's left and see how it goes. Thanks so much for helping me clean up."

It had taken over an hour to get Laura's stall back up and running, then Lilly left her to go back to her tea shop. She needed to see if Stacey and James needed any help.

As she navigated her way through the vendors and back out onto the row where the shop was, she heard sirens, and by the time she got there, she found an ambulance parked outside. She hurried over and, to her relief, found Stacey and James standing outside the door.

"What's happened?"

"I was helping a customer out to her car with a purchase when I saw a man had passed out on the pavement over there," Stacey said, pointing to the back of the row of vendors. "So I called an ambulance."

"Who is it?" she asked, approaching the paramedics, who were lifting a loaded stretcher.

A Frosty Combination

Her heart thumped as she briefly looked at the man they were carrying before one of them pulled up the blanket to cover his head.

"I'm sorry," one of the paramedics said to her, obviously recognising her shock and distress. "I'm afraid he's dead. Did you know him?"

Lilly nodded. "Yes. His name is Montgomery Douglas."

Chapter Five

BONNIE ARRIVED AT the scene not long after Lilly and after having a quiet word with the paramedics began to look around the immediate area where Monty's body had been found, trying to assess what had happened.

She crouched down and with gloved hands picked up one of the familiar take out mugs belonging to the Agony Aunt's café. She put it in an evidence bag and scoured the area for anything else. Retrieving only a couple of discarded chocolate wrappers and half a sandwich, she stood up when there was nothing more.

"I wonder if he had a heart attack or maybe a stroke?" Bonnie said to herself and jumped when James answered her. She turned to find him standing right behind her.

"Yes, I thought as much myself. You know, I thought I recognised him for a moment. What did you say his name was?"

"Montgomery Douglas," Lilly said. "Abigail's ex-husband."

"Oh, good heavens, of course. I didn't realise he was Abigail's former spouse. I should have put two and two together."

"Do you know him?" Bonnie asked.

"Not well. He works at the same university as I do, but in a different department, so our paths rarely cross. I'm sorry to say he's not a good sort."

"Stacey." Bonnie turned to the young girl. "Can you tell me exactly what happened?"

"Sure. I'd helped a customer carry a big box to her car, we sold one of the holly berry tea sets. When I came back I saw him lying over there, part hidden underneath the tarpaulin of the stall. I shook him to try to wake him up, I thought maybe he was drunk, but when he didn't respond I ran inside and called an ambulance."

"Did you see him when you came out the first time?"

Stacey shook her head. "No, I was talking to the customer and wasn't looking in that direction. I wished I'd seen him earlier."

"It wouldn't have made any difference, Stacey. He was already dead at that point," Bonnie said.

"Do think it was some sort of aneurysm?" Lilly asked. "Tom punched him hard on his temple, and he had a nasty tumble when they both crashed into Laura's stall. And he had that bad cut on his head."

Bonnie nodded thoughtfully. "It's possible, although I'm sure the cut to his head was from the glass. It was fairly superficial, I noticed once the bleeding had stopped. But the clout to the head might have caused some internal damage.

Especially if there was already some underlying problem which we're not aware of. We'll know more when the pathologist does his examination." She turned to Stacey's father. "James, you don't seem to hold your colleague in high regard. Is there a particular reason?"

James scowled and folded his arms. "I really don't know him well, but he has garnered a very poor reputation at the university."

"Go on."

"It was two or three months ago now. I happened to overhear a conversation between some of my female students about his behavior. It appeared they were talking about sexual harassment toward them by Monty Douglas. I had no choice but to intervene and ask them about it. It's a serious allegation and would result in immediate dismissal and possible charges. It appeared he had made several inappropriate comments to a particular girl during one of his lectures. Once she'd come forward and shared her experience, the others also admitted he'd been lewd and indecent toward them as well."

"Did you confront him, dad?" Stacey asked.

"No, that wasn't my place. I did, however, report him and as a result there was an internal investigation started. It's still ongoing as far as I know. Unfortunately, word spread that it was me who had reported him, so naturally he found out. He made my life as miserable as possible after that."

"He sounds like a despicable piece of work," Lilly said. "Wait. Does Abigail know what has happened?"

"I doubt it," Bonnie said, shaking her head. "I didn't even know it was Monty until I got here. You'd better tell her before she finds out from someone else, though. Listen,

I'm going to have to leave the stall to you now, Lilly. I want to get to the mortuary and see if I can expedite the autopsy. I need to know what we're dealing with here."

"Of course, Bonnie. I wouldn't expect you to stay. You need to do your proper job now. Thanks for all the help you have given us."

"You're welcome. Thanks, Lilly, see you later." Bonnie said and disappeared into the crowd.

Lilly turned to Stacey and James. "I think we can begin to close the shop now. It's almost time anyway. They'll be wanting to set up the live music events. I'll go back to the stalls and help clear those. I need to tell Abigail what has happened."

"Poor Abigail," Stacey said. "I hope she's not too upset."

Lilly set off back to the stalls with a heavy heart. She had no idea how Abigail was going to react.

"Hi," she said as she approached.

"Hey, what happened? Bonnie ran off about an hour ago and never came back. Is everything all right?" Abigail asked.

"Archie, Rodney, could you two cope here for a minute? I need to talk with Abigail." Both men nodded and Lilly took Abigail's arm and guided her to a relatively quiet space.

"Abigail, I'm sorry to have to tell you this news. Monty was found collapsed outside the tea shop earlier. We don't know what happened yet, but he was dead by the time he was discovered."

Abigail looked at her quizzically. "What? I don't understand. He was fine before. Are you positive it's Monty?"

"Yes, it's definitely him. I know it doesn't make sense at the moment, but there will need to be an autopsy. Bonnie is on her way now. It could be any number of things. A heart attack or a stoke, or an aneurysm. He had been in a fight earlier after all."

"Idiot," Abigail said, shaking her head. "I don't know what to say, Lilly. I mean, I cared about him once, but he made my life miserable the whole time I was with him. Then to come here and harass me the way he did? I know it sounds awful, but all I can feel at the moment is relief. I was starting to be afraid of what he might do. Even if he had left Plumpton Mallet today like Bonnie demanded, who's to say he wouldn't be back tomorrow, or next week or next year? I would have been living my life constantly looking over my shoulder. I'm a little sad, I suppose, but more because it's as though his entire life was just a waste. Pointless. He didn't achieve anything, only made other people's lives wretched. I must admit, I feel like I'm finally free for the first time in years."

Chapter Six

IF THE PLUMPTON Mallet Christmas market was the epitome of a magical and fresh winter wonderland, a couple of days later, on the Monday morning, it was the complete opposite. The snow had melted and become a muddy, dirty slush and then had frozen overnight to form sheets of grubby black ice all over the town. It was bitterly cold, made worse by the biting, icy wind which sneaked under your collar and cuffs and froze your ears and nose.

Lilly loaded up the car with Earl in his carrier, her bike now safely stored in the shed for the winter, and started her careful journey to work. In the town car-park at the rear of the row of shops, she lifted the carrier and got an indignant yowl from Earl, who didn't like the sudden change in temperature at all.

"It's only for a minute, Earl," Lilly said. "Then you'll be tucked up nice and warm in the window."

As Lilly let herself in the back entrance to avoid walking round the block on the treacherous ice, she found the shop was already up and running. This was the beauty of having your manager living in the flat above.

"Good morning, Stacey," Lilly said, freeing Earl. He immediately streaked across the shop floor, effortlessly jumping into the window, and was curled up in his basket within seconds. Lilly laughed. "That cat really hates the cold."

"Good morning, Lilly. It's most likely because he had to live on the streets for so long. I assume he still remembers what it was like," a voice said, its owner popping up from behind the counter.

"James, what are you doing here?" she asked, surprised to see him.

"Stacey had a college related emergency so left me to man the fort. I hope you don't mind? She shouldn't belong."

"Why on earth should I mind? You're doing a superb job. Quite frankly, you are one of the team now whether you like it or not. So much so that you're included in the Secret Santa."

"I rather think that's because it was my daughter's idea," he said, laughing. "I have no idea what to get Frederick... oh, good grief, I wasn't supposed to say that, was I?"

Lilly laughed at the look of horror on his face. "Well, no, you weren't, but never mind. So, you're now obligated to buy something for your daughter's boyfriend?"

"Yes, I know. It's awful, but I don't even know what sort of things he likes. I rather wish I'd pulled another name from the pot if I'm honest."

I know what you mean, she thought with amusement. Then she saw an opportunity. "What sort of thing would you like to receive? Perhaps that will help you work out something suitable for Fred."

"I doubt it," he mused. "We're not very much alike. Not to mention the obvious age gap. But I do realise this will give me a better chance to get to know him. I'm relatively new to this whole 'dad' thing, as you know. I just want to make sure I treat him well, too. He means a lot to Stacey, and he looks after her very well."

So much for that bright idea, Lilly thought. James hadn't given anything away about his own likes and dislikes. "My advice would be to treat him as you would Stacey. Perhaps part son, part friend? Fred is a really lovely young man, and he dotes on your daughter."

"Yes, that's a good idea. Oh, I almost forgot, Laura Smith dropped this in for you," James said, ducking behind the counter and retrieving a small box wrapped in dark green paper with a red bow.

"My ornament," Lilly said, excitedly.

She unwrapped it and took out the bauble. Not only had Laura repaired the sharp edge of the damaged ear, she'd added some colour to make it look more like Earl himself. She'd even added a small tag to the cat's collar with the initials *EG* etched into the glass. "Oh, my word, it's perfect," she said.

"That's your cat," James said, as Lilly dangled the ornament from the red ribbon. "Isn't it clever? It looks just like him."

Lilly took the ornament to the bay window and hung it on the side of the Christmas tree, which faced the market square so anyone passing by would see it. "Now we have a cat in both windows," she said with a grin. She paused to check the agony aunt basket, which was full of fliers and the odd bit of rubbish stuffed through by the various tourists who'd come for the Christmas market. It happened to many of the shops every year, even though the council put out extra refuse bins for the event. She scrunched them up, ready to put them in the bin. In among the detritus was a hand-written letter. "It looks as though I've received an agony aunt letter. I haven't had one in a while."

"I expect the new logo yesterday helped to remind people," James said. "There could be a few more in the future."

"That's more than possible," Lilly agreed, then joined James behind the counter. The day was about to begin.

LILLY HEARD THE storeroom door open and Stacey rushed in. "You made it," James said. "Good timing."

"I'm so sorry," Stacey said to Lilly. "I got an email from my professor saying I'd left my bag in his office and he was leaving today for Christmas vacation. I had to run over and get it before he left."

"It's really not a problem, Stacey. It was an emergency. Besides, your dad was here."

"Thanks for understanding. I think I've been a little scatter brained this week with everything going on."

"I wouldn't have known it. I couldn't have done everything you managed to do in time for market day. In fact, without you, I doubt we'd have had a stall at all. Plus those take away mugs you designed and organised were fabulous. Everybody loved them. Did you know we now have a waiting list for more and people are talking about collecting any others you design? And you helped train all the staff and put the work schedule together. You're allowed to be a bit scatterbrained, Stacey, you've earned it."

"I try," Stacey said, taking over from her father behind the counter.

The front door opened and Lilly looked up to see another familiar face. Archie Brown walked in, rubbing his hands and shivering, muttering about the frigid temperatures and how the pavement was like an ice rink.

"Hi, Archie. I didn't expect to see you today. I've just got a pot of tea ready. You look like you need thawing out. Want one?"

"Now you're talking," Archie said, taking a seat at the counter. "But you'd better put it in one of those plastic cups. I'm shaking so much I'll probably drop a china one. By the way, I bought a tea set yesterday, but my car was full of Christmas shopping. Rodney dropped it in here for me to collect today. It's in the back, apparently."

"I'll go and check," Stacey said, scurrying off.

While James and Archie struck up a conversation about Monty and the drama of the day before, Lilly took the opportunity to read the agony aunt letter she'd received.

Dear Agony Aunt,

I have acquired an unfortunate reputation that is affecting both my personal and professional lives.

I'm worried I will never be able to escape this. I have made mistakes in my life, but I want to do better. How can I show people I have changed, particularly in professional settings?

This was a difficult question for Lilly to answer considering the lack of context and more pertinent information, but she did her best to craft an appropriate and helpful response to send back to the local post office box address listed at the top of the page.

Stacey returned, carrying a heavy box, which she promptly placed on the counter in front of Archie. "You bought one of our sunflower tea sets, too? We sold quite a few of those yesterday."

"I like it. I have a cousin who adores sunflowers, and I just found out her daughter broke her favourite teapot. She's a little tyke and a tad heavy handed," Archie said and laughed. "Her husband has been looking for a new set for her Christmas present, and I sent him a picture of yours. He asked me to get it for him before you sold out. I'll be driving up to give it to him today. I daresay he'll be earning some serious brownie points from his wife as a result."

"That's a lovely thing to do, Archie," Lilly said, looking up from her letter. "Is it a long drive for you?"

"Unfortunately, it is a bit of a haul, actually," he replied with a rueful smile. "And I had a lot to do today. I wanted to look into Monty's case for my next article."

"Case?" Stacey asked.

Archie looked from one to the other. "Haven't you heard? Monty was poisoned. It's a murder inquiry now."

A FROSTY COMBINATION

"**P**OISONED?" LILLY EXCLAIMED. "You mean somebody deliberately killed him?"

Archie nodded. "According to my source at the mortuary, yes. Although they've yet to identify the poison used. Another murder in Plumpton Mallet, would you believe it? We'll be getting a reputation as the Northern version of Midsomer before long."

"What a dreadful world we live in sometimes," James said sadly.

"Indeed," Archie said. "Though, and don't any of you repeat this, especially not to Abigail. I think the world is probably better off without a man like that. I haven't begun to scratch the surface of my research yet, but I've already learned enough to know the type of man he was and it fair turns my stomach, as well as making my blood boil."

"Yes, I'm sure there's quite a few at university who'll not miss him either," James said.

"That's right, you worked with him, didn't you?"

"At the same place, but not with him as such. However, I really don't want anything in the newspaper about my knowing him, Archie. The university understandably abhor bad press, and if it came out I not only knew him, but happened to be working in the very shop at the very time he was found outside, I'd have a lot of questions to answer. Particularly as it is well known he and I don't, or didn't rather, see eye to eye ever since I reported him."

"I won't mention you," Archie promised. "But, I was going to contact the university today to see if I could get some more information about Monty's sexual harassment accusation. I expect I'll get the runaround and they will remain tight-lipped about the whole thing. Like you say, they don't like bad press. If I come up against the proverbial brick wall, I might have to come back to you for the information. Anonymously, of course," Archie said to James.

"I understand, Archie, but I'm not sure I can do that. They are my employer after all and I happen to love my job. Let me think about it if you would?"

Lilly knew that Archie would do his utmost to get the information he needed from the university itself, but in all probability, he would come back empty handed. She felt a little sorry for James. When Archie got the bit between his teeth while researching an article, he could be relentless.

"The way Monty treated Abigail was really bad, too," Stacey added to the conversation.

"I've heard about that," Archie said.

"Hopefully, you've heard enough that you won't need to bother Abigail," Lilly said.

"Don't worry, Lilly. Abigail and I were hardly going to be best friends, but I never let my personal feelings influence a story. Besides, I'm not nearly so angry with her as I once was. Not now I know what she's been through. Anyway, I have what I need in that regard from other sources, there's no need for me to interview her."

Lilly was relieved. After everything that had happened, she knew Abigail wouldn't want to have the press hounding her as well.

Chapter Seven

THE SHOP DOOR opened, and Bonnie walked in, briefcase in hand. She smiled as she saw them all gathered around the counter, Archie with his nose in a box checking the tea set for his cousin.

"Good morning," Lilly said. "Archie has just informed us Monty's death is now a murder investigation. How are you holding up? Do you want a cup of tea?"

"I'd love one. Anything you've got brewed is fine. I just need something to permeate the chill in my bones. It's absolutely freezing out there," Bonnie said, taking a seat at the counter. "And yes, Monty was murdered. It makes it all the more difficult because he wasn't local."

"I heard he was poisoned," Archie said. "Is that right?"

Bonnie nodded. "I'm afraid so. The poison was discovered in the take away mug I found next to the body."

"What?" Lilly said, aghast. "Someone put poison in one of our drinks? No one else has been poisoned, have they?"

"Not as far as we know," Bonnie said. "And I believe we would have heard by now, as it obviously was a fast acting poison. I don't think it was put directly in the pot you served from, Lilly, so don't worry about that. No, whatever was used was put directly into Monty's mug."

"And you don't know the type of poison yet?"

"Not at the moment. I'm waiting to hear the results of the tests. It's more complicated as far as the investigation goes because he's not local and no one knew him. As far as we are aware, until this week he'd never even visited Plumpton Mallet. Which brings me to the reason I'm here. We need to go with what knowledge we do have. James, would you be willing to let me take your fingerprints?"

James raised an eyebrow. "My fingerprints? I'm not a suspect, am I?"

Bonnie smiled wryly. "I doubt it was you, James, but we do need to eliminate you. You knew Monty, and he was found outside the shop where you were working at the time."

"So, this is to rule James out. I understand that," Lilly said. "But you need to compare his fingerprints with something you already have, don't you? What is it?"

"No flies on you is there, Miss Tweed?" Bonnie replied with a sigh. "All right, keep it between ourselves, please. We found a set of additional prints on the mug. Not Monty's, obviously, but they may belong to the killer."

"Well, that's a solid start," Archie said, reaching for his pen and notebook.

"That's off the record, Archie Brown. I better not see anything mentioning fingerprints in the paper tomorrow. This is an open investigation and I can't afford to make any mistakes. Especially not so early in the process. You know I'll give you what I can when I can. And when it's safe for the public to know."

"Whatever you say, detective," Archie said with a mock salute.

"So, what do I have to do?" James said.

Bonnie plonked her briefcase on the counter. "Sorry, but our digital fingerprint scanner is not working at the moment, so I'll have to do this the old fashioned way, I'm afraid." James sighed and rolled up his sleeve.

"Why can't we wait until the scanner is fixed?" James asked. "This stuff looks as though it will take ages to wash off." He had a scowl on his face while Bonnie pressed each of his fingers into the ink pad and transferred them to the waiting card. He didn't get a reply, so when Bonnie had finished, he went into the back storeroom to scrub his hands.

He'd sounded quite annoyed and Lilly couldn't really blame him. She felt as though Bonnie was using her friendship with them to avoid answering James' questions. And to fingerprint him in the middle of the shop where any customer could have walked in and seen it? Not that there had been any, the weather being what it was. But still, it wasn't the usual way of doing things and Lilly couldn't help but feel slightly annoyed with Bonnie.

"I'll see you out, Bonnie," Lilly said, when she realised she'd already packed up her kit and was about to leave.

"Okay. Stacey, please thank your dad for me. I know it was an inconvenience."

"Will do," Stacey replied, and Lilly could tell she wasn't very happy either, although she was doing a very good job of hiding it. Lilly could only imagine how Stacey felt watching her father being fingerprinted in front of her. She followed Bonnie to the door, opened it and they both sheltered in front of the shop, huddled together.

"All right, Bonnie, what's really going on? Why do you need James' fingerprints?"

"Because he's one of the few people here who actually knew him."

"I don't think that's the whole story, Bonnie. Do you actually suspect him of killing Monty?"

Bonnie sighed. "I've got to get these fingerprints to the lab, Lilly. If you want to talk, then let's do it later, all right?"

"How about over lunch?" Lilly said. "I need to go and check on how things are at the café, anyway."

"Yes, okay. I'll see you there later."

Lilly returned inside to the welcome warmth of the shop. If anything, the temperature outside appeared to have fallen even further. Archie stayed for a little while longer, but eventually had to get on the road to deliver the tea set to his cousin, otherwise he'd be driving in the dark. Not a good idea with sub-zero temperatures and icy roads.

The shop wasn't busy that morning. Nearly everybody had attended the market and stocked up, and the weather was obviously keeping most people indoors. The three of them spent their time replenishing the shop stock, then Lilly went to the storeroom to start packing up the various orders she'd received. The majority of the orders were her special Christmas blend. She was pleased it was so popular, she'd worked hard on getting the balance of flavours just right. As she was getting ready to tie the parcels, Stacey joined her.

"It's not busy in the shop and my dad is stewing in there. Do you need some help?"

"Of course, thank you," Lilly replied, handing her the twine.

The job went much faster with two people and Stacey took them back into the shop, ready for collection, while Lilly cleared away. Checking the clock, she realised it was almost time for lunch. She returned to the shop and found James with Earl. It seemed the cat was helping him to calm down a little.

"Do you want to give me your lunch orders? I've a few things to take care of at the café, but I'll bring it back for you."

Stacey hastily scribbled down their requirements and Lilly, wrapped up in her thickest winter coat, with scarf and gloves on and her hood pulled so tight hardly any of her face was showing, left to keep her loosely arranged lunch appointment with Bonnie. She hoped she would turn up and not make an excuse. She knew very well Lilly was intending to question her.

WHEN SHE ARRIVED, she was told Abigail was in the office working on the books, so Lilly didn't disturb her. Instead, she found a seat in one of the booths and waited for Bonnie. She didn't have to wait long. Bonnie entered, her feet dragging as she scanned the café and found Lilly. She shook off her jacket and took a seat opposite, picking up the menu as a diversion tactic. When she put it down, Lilly spoke.

"So, what's really going on?"

"Oh, come on, Lilly," Bonnie groaned. "Let me at least get a coffee before you start grilling me."

"I'm not going to let it lie, Bonnie," Lilly said. "You should know me better than that. I don't see you marching in here and taking Abigail's prints, and she was the one most hurt by Monty."

"It wasn't Abigail. She was either at the stall, with me, or another person the entire time. It's impossible for her to have done it."

"All right, but what about Tom? Was he in a cell all night or was he released before Monty was found dead?"

"He'd already been released actually, but he wouldn't have had time to poison Monty as far as we can ascertain."

"So why are you singling out James?"

Bonnie paused until the waitress came and took their order, then spoke quietly.

"Look, Monty was found outside the tea shop where James was working. Monty's take away mug had your tea in it. James admits to knowing the victim and Monty had been making James' life at the university miserable. Everyone else was either busy working on the stalls, or, as in the case of Tom, in a cell at the police station. James had both motive and opportunity, Lilly. But, if his fingerprints aren't a match, then I'll move on."

"All right, but what aren't you telling me?"

Bonnie rolled her eyes. "Crikey, you're persistent today. All right, I telephoned the university earlier. There was an incident between James and Monty a couple of weeks ago. It sounds as though there's more to this than James is admitting. Something happened. I don't know all the details yet but I will find out, Lilly."

Lilly rubbed her hands over her face in frustration. She couldn't believe it was James who had killed Monty. But then again, how well did she actually know him? It was true she hadn't taken to him at first, mainly because of the way he'd treated Stacey. But that was all in the past. Now he was doing his level best to be a good father, to make up for all his previous absences. Surely he wouldn't jeopardise all that due to an argument with a colleague?

She shook her head and tried not to think about it. All she wanted to do was enjoy lunch with her friend. They both tucked into their food, but didn't talk very much. Bonnie was obviously thinking about the case, and Lilly was doing her best to forget it.

They chatted briefly about how well both the café and the tea shop stalls had done at the market, even with all the drama, and Bonnie told her she'd had Laura fill in an official accident report so she could get it sent off to the insurance company as soon as possible.

"That was good of you," Lilly said. Then she remembered Bonnie was one of the good guys. Lilly knew her friend and understood the things she was doing and why. She might not agree with her methods, but she would solve the case, she was sure of it. Whoever had killed Monty deserved to be caught and sentenced.

"Thank you for sharing with me what you could," she said, when they'd finished their lunch and Lilly was holding Stacey and James' lunch bags.

"I need you to promise it will remain just between us, Lilly."

"But surely Stacey and James have a right to know what's going on?"

Bonnie shook her head. "He's our prime suspect at the moment, and obviously the case is still under investigation. I'm sorry. I shouldn't have told you what I did, but the reason I did was because I trust you. Please don't break that trust, Lilly, this case is difficult enough as it is."

Lilly sighed. "I won't, Bonnie. I do understand and I'll keep quiet, but please let me know what's going on when you can, okay? See you later." she said. And the two women parted ways.

"YOU JUST MISSED a lovely customer," Stacey said when she returned to the shop a few minutes later. "They wanted to say how much they loved your holiday tea. They've just purchased several boxes for friends and family as gifts."

"I'm glad they enjoyed it."

"And another customer wanted to know why we were stocking the Agony Aunt's café tee shirts. I told them how they are connected and they thought the logo was great."

"Well, we have a terrific designer," Lilly replied, and watched Stacey's cheeks turn pink.

"Is that lunch?"

Lilly said it was and suggested she and James eat together in the back room. As they disappeared, she felt Earl rubbing against her ankles and took him to Stacey. She'd give him his lunch while Lilly helped a couple who had just entered.

"Welcome. Can I help at all?"

"I would absolutely love to buy the little village holiday set, but I see you've sold out," the young woman said in a disappointed voice. "My aunt would adore it. I was going to purchase one at your market stall yesterday, but I got distracted and by the time I returned they'd all gone."

"Don't worry, I actually placed another order this morning. They'll be here tomorrow after lunch. Can you come back then?"

The young man stepped forward. "Would it be possible for you to post it directly to our aunt with a card from us? I'd hate to pack it myself and discover it has broken at the other end."

"Of course," Lilly said. "Come back tomorrow afternoon and I'll take all the information from you and you can choose a gift card." She took down their names and a telephone number and they left. By that time, James and Stacey were back in the shop. An hour or so later, Stacey mentioned she had a bit of homework she needed to do.

"I can do it in the back in case you need me?"

"Don't worry, you go home, Stacey, and get your work done. It's quiet today, anyway."

Stacey thanked her and disappeared upstairs to her flat. With just her and James left, Lilly hoped she could get some idea of what to get him for the Secret Santa, however, James didn't want to talk. Lilly could sense he was angry and frustrated and probably a bit humiliated. She asked him if he wanted to go home?

"I suppose I'm not the best company at the moment," he said. "I was just caught unawares this morning."

"I understand. Look, there's only a couple of hours to go before we close and I can deal with it. You go home, take some tea with you. Mint, chamomile, lavender, rose or matcha, all help with stress and anxiety. Just take what you need."

James thanked her profusely, chose a mint and lavender blend as well as a matcha and, after wrapping up warmly, also left. The cold wind blowing through the shop for a minute as he opened and closed the door. Lilly hoped nothing adverse would come of James' fingerprints. He and Stacey had become so close over the previous months, and they didn't need anything getting in the way. Lilly settled down and drank a cup of Rose Petal Raspberry tea. She needed a moment of Zen herself.

There were no more customers that day, so Lilly was ready when the time came to go home. She put Earl in his carrier, locked up, then even more carefully than she had that morning, because of the failing light, drove home.

She fed them both, then settled in front of the blazing fire to watch the television. The local news was covering the death of a man found at the Plumpton Mallet Christmas Market, although Monty hadn't been named nor had the fact it was murder. Lilly turned the television off. Surely James would not have killed Monty. What was the point? And what possible motive could he have? She curled up on the sofa with Earl at her feet purring softly, and drifted off to sleep, still wondering what gift she could get for James, and knowing it would need to be something extra special considering what he was going through.

Chapter Eight

THE FOLLOWING MORNING, Lilly drove to the shop earlier than usual. Stacey was in a class all morning, so that left Rodney to open up the shop. While Rodney had proved to be an excellent employee, he didn't have Stacey's experience, and she didn't want to make it a habit to leave her staff to do the lion's share of the work. Stacey had proven herself ten times over and was more than capable of managing the tea shop and the café, but at the moment, she wasn't so sure of Rodney. He'd not been with them long enough, and she didn't want to leave him without any help or support.

Again, she parked in the rear town car-park, bundled up in her coat already, she just added her scarf, hat and gloves, then picked up Earl's carrier. He meowed once they were in the chilly air, which was his habit.

"I know with your fur and your luxury carrier, you're definitely warmer than I am, Earl," she said. "So you can stop your complaining for one minute while I get to the shop. Have you forgotten you used to be a stray young man? I'm sure you've spent more than one winter outside, so I know you're tougher than you're making out. Now, relax, we're here." Which was a good job, as several people had glanced in her direction and one or two had given her a wide berth. They obviously thought she was a little mad having a full-blown conversation with her cat.

Lilly had walked around the block and entered the shop through the front door and was pleased to see the Christmas tree all lit up in the front window. The shelves were re-stocked and the place was polished to a shine.

Well done, Rodney, she thought, then immediately heard apologies as the front door opened again.

"I'm so sorry I'm late, Lilly," she spun round to find Rodney entering. Did that mean Stacey had set up the shop before she'd left for college? No, surely not.

"Are you just arriving now?" she asked.

"Yes, my car stalled," he said, panting. "It really hates starting in cold weather. Took me ages to get it going."

"Then who set the shop up if you weren't here?" she asked, and Rodney looked around and shrugged.

"I don't know, it wasn't me. Although I wish I could take the credit. It looks as though everything has been dusted too."

Lilly let Earl out of his carrier so he could bolt to his bed in the window, then divested herself of her cold weather clothing. Behind the counter, she checked the drawers, as was her habit, and found them all fully stocked.

"Good morning," a voice said, and Lilly turned to find James exiting the storeroom.

"James. What are you doing here at this time?"

"I've been staying with Stacey upstairs, remember?"

"Well, I know that," she laughed. "But what are you doing in the shop? Did you do all this?" she asked, waving an arm to take in the pristine premises.

"All what?" he asked. "Oh, the preparation work before we open, you mean? Yes. I awoke when Stacey left for college, so as I was already here I thought I'd make myself useful. It's all right, isn't it?"

"Of course it is. It's wonderful, in fact. Thank you, James."

"You're welcome. I enjoyed it actually. I don't have much to do while Stacey's at college and it was lovely and peaceful setting things up in the quiet."

Already people were starting to enter so Lilly asked Rodney to man the till while she chatted with the customers about their requirements and James brewed the holiday tea for people to sample.

They'd not been open an hour when Bonnie turned up, and the look on her face as well as the constable who followed her in behind told Lilly this wasn't a social call.

"BONNIE? IS EVERYTHING all right?" she asked.

"I need to talk with James," she said in an official tone Lilly rarely heard, bypassing her friend before insisting James accompany her outside.

It was with a feeling of gnawing sense of uneasiness that Lilly watched the conversation through the shop door window.

She could see them talking, politely at first, but whatever friendly encounter James had expected initially turned sour very quickly. "Are you out of your mind?" she heard him say as his voice raised. Lilly couldn't hear what Bonnie's reply was, but before she knew he was being escorted to the rear of the police car parked outside.

"Oh, no!" Lilly exclaimed. "Rodney, watch the shop," she shouted, not waiting for a response before bolting outside. "Bonnie, what on earth are you doing? You can't seriously be arresting James?"

"Lilly," James called out. "When Stacey gets back from college, tell her to call my solicitor immediately. She has the number. Explain what's happened," he pleaded, before Bonnie slammed the door shut, cutting him off.

"Bonnie, for heavens' sake, please don't do this. You can't possibly think James is guilty of killing Monty."

The few customers who had been in the shop and witnessed James being hauled outside by the police trickled out, followed by a shocked Rodney. "What on earth, Bonnie?" was all he managed to say, unknowingly echoing Lilly's immediate reaction.

Bonnie moved closer to Lilly. "We've got the fingerprint results back. They were James' on that take away mug Monty drank the poison from."

"Fine, but that doesn't mean James added the poison, Bonnie," Lilly argued. "He could have just served him from the tea shop. I wouldn't be surprised if all our prints are on those mugs. We all must have handled them at one point or another."

"It's more than just the prints, Lilly. I can't go into any detail at present, but there's more between James and Monty than he said. I've received confirmation from the university there was a violent, physical confrontation between the two of them. Monty wasn't the only one who was in danger of losing his tenure, Lilly."

"Are you saying James lied about what happened?"

"I'm saying he omitted to tell the full truth," Bonnie answered.

"Which is not the same thing at all, Bonnie." Lilly said angrily. "Not wanting to reveal his personal business doesn't mean he killed the man. This is ludicrous."

"And when would he have had the time to do it?" Rodney asked. Both Lilly and Bonnie had been unaware he'd been listening. "He was here with Stacey all day, wasn't he? He's hardly going to poison someone in front of his daughter, is he?"

"Christmas Market day was exceptionally busy," Bonnie said, unmoved by Rodney's logic. "It's entirely possible he slipped something into Monty's drink without anyone noticing. Monty was found dead outside this shop. He had a vendetta with James. James' prints are all over the poisoned mug, and as of this minute, James is under arrest. Despite how that might make my friends feel, I can't let it get in the way of me doing my job." Bonnie started to walk back to the car.

"Wait," Lilly said. "Did you find out what type of poison it was?"

"Cyanide."

"Cyanide?" Lilly exclaimed. "Where would James have got cyanide from, Bonnie? Think about it. It's not as though I keep a vat of the stuff in the store room."

"I don't know, Lilly, and sarcasm doesn't really help you know? Right now, it looks as though he obviously got it from somewhere. He'll get a chance to defend himself in court. Now, I need to get back to the station." Bonnie sighed and looked at Lilly one last time. "I'm sorry, Lilly. Please apologise to Stacey for me too. I know she'll be angry with me when she finds out."

"She's not the only one, Bonnie," Lilly said with feeling. "You've got it wrong, you know. And I think Stacey deserves an apology from you directly."

Bonnie said nothing more, but gave Lilly a remorseful look as she got in the car and drove James away.

"THIS ISN'T RIGHT," Lilly said as she stamped her feet to try to get her blood pumping again. "There's not enough proper evidence, if you ask me. And whatever it is Bonnie thinks she's got is all circumstantial. The whole thing is ridiculous. I'm shocked that Bonnie has gone as far as she has. I can't fathom out what she was thinking."

"I don't know, Lilly," Rodney said, rubbing the back of his head anxiously.

"Don't tell me you think James is guilty as well?" Lilly said more sharply than she'd intended.

"No, of course I don't," he replied, raising his hands in a defensive gesture and taking a step back. "All I'm saying is when you add everything up, it's quite damning for James. Bonnie doesn't really have a choice but to follow it all up. It's her job."

"This is a total nightmare," she said.

Rodney lightly touched her arm. "We should go back inside. It's freezing out here. And the forecast has said we're due for more snow."

Lilly nodded and followed him back into the warmth of the shop. All she could think about was Stacey. Currently, she was sitting in class without a care in the world, about to end the term so she could spend the first Christmas she could remember with her father. She glanced up at the old clock. Stacey would be finished in an hour and a half. "I'm going to go and meet Stacey out of college," she told Rodney. "I want to tell her face to face about what's happened. I don't want her to find out from anyone but me. And I don't want her driving while she's upset. The roads are treacherous enough without adding emotion into the mix."

"That's probably a good idea. Do you want some Lavender tea?"

"Thank you, Rodney, yes, please. I need to be calm as possible when I tell Stacey her father has been arrested for murder. And right at this moment I'm as angry as I ever have been."

Chapter Nine

THE SNOW WHICH Rodney said had been forecast was beginning to fall in earnest as Lilly left the shop, and she pulled up the hood of her coat and wrapped her scarf tightly around her lower face while she attempted a dash to her car. They were great fluffy flakes, the kind that settle almost immediately and cloak everything in a winter wonderland display. However, the wind was whipping them around in a chaotic frenzy and Lilly found it was more akin to walking through a vortex of white, making it difficult to keep a sense of direction. Thank goodness she knew the town like the back of her hand. At the Christmas market, the snow had added to the magical ambiance, but today, with the pall of murder hanging over her, it felt ominous and suffocating.

She started the car engine, turning the heater to full blast while she waited for the wipers to clear the windscreen. She sat for a moment to collect her thoughts before leaving the car-park and decided being blunt about what had happened would be the best approach. Stacey wouldn't appreciate her trying to sugar-coat the news. Not that there was a way to make the arrest of her father sound more positive.

Lilly found herself gripping the steering wheel extra tightly and clenching her teeth as she thought furiously about what Bonnie had done. She took a deep breath and willed herself to calm down. Like Rodney had said, Bonnie was just following what little evidence she had because it was her only choice. "Well," she said. "I'll just have to try and prove James is innocent. And that means finding out who the real killer is."

After an excruciatingly slow drive to the university, which made Lilly grateful she'd set off in plenty of time, she circled the car-park until she found Stacey's car, then parked in the adjoining space and waited for her to arrive. She saw her ten minutes later cautiously negotiating the snow-laden steps and got out of her vehicle to wait for her.

Stacey approached her with a huge grin on her face, then Lilly saw concern etched in her features as she realised something must be wrong for Lilly to be at the university waiting for her. "Hey, Lilly. Is everything all right? Has something happened?"

"Bonnie came to the shop this morning, Stacey. I'm so sorry, but she's arrested your dad. His fingerprints were on the mug she found by Monty's body."

"What?" she said, shaking her head as though she couldn't quite process what she was being told. Then her chin began to quiver. "No, that's not right, dad didn't do it! Is he all right? Where is he?"

Lilly gave the girl a hug. "He's at the police station being interviewed. He wants you to call his solicitor. He said you had the number?"

Stacey nodded. "It's in my phone."

"I came so I could drive you back home. I don't think it's a good idea for you to drive at the moment."

Stacey shook her head. Lilly could see she was holding it together better than she'd expected her to, but it was by a thread and as soon as reality hit, she'd probably break down. "No, it's okay. Thanks, but I'd rather drive myself. I don't want to have to come back for my car."

Lilly thought for a moment, then acquiesced. With the snow falling as heavily as it was, it might be some time before they could come back for Stacey's car. "All right, but I'll follow you. The roads are treacherous underneath this new snow. Go carefully and if you need to stop, do so. I'll be right behind you."

Stacey nodded and got in her car. Once she'd pulled out, Lilly did the same and the two of them made a laboriously slow journey back to the car-park in the town centre. They walked in silence back to the shop and entered just as Rodney was saying goodbye to a customer. Once they were alone, Rodney approached Stacey.

"I'm sorry about what has happened, Stacey. How are you doing?"

Lilly could tell Stacey had cried in the car on the way back. Her eyes were red and slightly swollen, as was her nose.

Now, though, it seemed she'd got it out of her system and was beginning to get angry at the injustice.

"I'm fine, just shocked. I can't believe Bonnie did this."

"I know," Rodney said. "Me neither. There's no way your dad did this."

"No, he didn't. And you know what? My money's on Abigail," she snapped angrily.

"Stacey!" Lilly exclaimed in surprise, although she knew the words were spoken from frustration and bitterness.

"Oh, come on, Lilly," Stacey said. "Abigail has the biggest motive. We all know that. Monty was harassing her and he abused her while they were married. Then he turns up here when she thought she'd escaped him. She was probably scared out of her mind and wanted to get rid of him. I know I sure wouldn't want to spend the rest of my life looking over my shoulder." She sighed. "Look, I know it's mean to think it, but it makes sense. Do you not remember how crazy she used to act? She almost pushed you off a ladder! Maybe she just snapped."

"I know that, Stacey," Lilly said gently. "But she was going through a considerable amount at the time. She's changed a lot since then."

"Yeah, but what she was going through was caused by Monty! And him being here may have brought out that side of her again. It's not like I would blame her. But seriously, don't you think it makes a lot more sense her killing Monty than my dad doing it?"

"That's a good point," Rodney said, with a sage nod. "I didn't know Abigail tried to push you off a ladder?"

"It didn't happen quite like that, Rodney," Lilly said testily, ending that avenue of discussion. "Stacey, we know James is innocent, but it doesn't mean we can start throwing accusations around. Abigail is our friend and my business partner and I don't believe she did it either. She was in full view of someone the whole time at the market. She just didn't have the opportunity. Look, what you need to do first is get hold of your father's solicitor. He urgently needs representation. And while you're doing that, I'm going to start looking into things."

Stacey half smiled. "Great. Our local super sleuth is on the case at last. Okay, you're right, I shouldn't start blaming anyone until we know more. It won't help anything. I'm going up to my flat to call my dad's solicitor."

"Thank you, Stacey. I'll go and have a chat with Abigail and see if she can tell me more about Monty. Rodney, will you be all right running the shop on your own?"

"I will. With the weather like it is, I doubt I'll be run off my feet."

"Thank you. And don't forget to feed Earl if I'm not back in time."

"And I'll only be upstairs if things get crazy," Stacey added. "I can take Earl up with me if you want?"

Rodney nodded, and Stacey scooped the dozy cat out of the window, hugging him close and disappeared to the flat upstairs.

For what seemed like the tenth time already that day, Lilly donned her winter coat, hat, scarf and gloves and walked down the street to the café. She knew Abigail was hard at work in the back room, the one they had designated to be a special tea room for events and parties. They hadn't managed to get it finished in time for the grand re-opening but with their first booking, a vintage afternoon tea to celebrate a Golden wedding anniversary, imminent they couldn't put it off any longer.

Her feet were like ice blocks by the time she entered the café, so she immediately ordered one of Abigail's peppermint orange cocoa's to help thaw herself out. Jean was working the barista shift that day and with her usual efficiency had a large beverage ready for Lilly before she could take off her gloves.

"Thank you, Jean," Lilly said, dropping a pound coin in the tip jar on the counter despite it being her own café. "Is Abigail in the tearoom?"

"She is," Jean replied, thanking Lilly for the tip.

Lilly approached the back of the café and was thrilled to see the new double sliding doors, with their wood floral carvings, had been installed since she'd last been inside. They looked absolutely stunning. She slid one open and stood on the threshold, her mouth agape.

"Wow," she said. They'd chosen a traditional art nouveau style for the tearoom and it looked a far cry from the damp, former storage space it had been when they'd taken over the premises. "Abigail, this is absolutely breathtaking," Lilly said, sliding the doors closed behind her. One accent wall had been done in Golden Lily, a William Morris design on an indigo background. There was a china display cabinet filled with Art

Nouveau tea sets and other vintage knick knacks. The wall sconces were stained glass effect with Charmlight bulbs in a soft Rose shade behind, and the top half of the painted walls were a soft green that perfectly matched the palest hue in the wallpaper, with wood panelling on the lower half.

As with the main café, the floors were hard wood, although this time in a slightly darker shade, and there were extra large faux ferns in huge Victorian pots. The ceiling pendants were Tiffany style with snowdrop shaped glass shades in green and soft yellow. And again, as with the café, there were two tall standard lamps in the corner with Tiffany style stained glass shades. To finish it off, several prints by Alphonse Mucha were hung at strategic points around the room, so that no matter where you were sitting, you had a view of something beautiful.

Abigail was currently looking through various tablecloth samples to see which would suit the interior. "Hi, Lilly. It does, doesn't it? I'm thrilled with how it's all come together."

"You must have been working day and night to achieve all this so quickly. I'm so sorry I wasn't here to help."

"It doesn't matter. I've enjoyed every single minute of it. To be honest, it's been an excellent distraction."

"How are you doing, Abigail?" Lilly asked, sitting at one of the bare dark oak tables where the table cloth samples lay.

Abigail joined her and shrugged. "As well as I can be, I suppose. I'm still finding it hard to believe. What do you think about these cloths? I thought of having two, one longer one underneath in the indigo, then a white, slightly shorter one over the top."

"That sounds perfect," Lilly said. "Abigail, have you heard the news about James?"

"James? No. Why, what's happened?"

"Bonnie arrested him for Monty's murder this morning."

"No!" Abigail said in horror. "Oh, Lilly, that's dreadful news. James didn't kill Monty. Why on earth would he? Oh, poor Stacey. Does she know?"

Lilly nodded. "She's putting a brave face on it, but she's very upset and angry as you can imagine."

"I don't understand what Bonnie was thinking," Abigail said.

"My sentiments exactly. I know it's a touchy subject, but could you tell me more about your ex-husband? Anything, no matter how incongruous it might seem. I'm trying to find something Bonnie may have missed that I could present to her so she'll release James. That's if you don't mind?"

"GOOD GRIEF, LILLY, you shouldn't need to ask. Of course I don't mind. We need to clear James' name. I'll do whatever I can to help you do that. I'm not sure what I can tell you that will be of use, but he was a reporter for quite a long time. A while after he left that job, he got tenure teaching journalism at a university down South. He lost that job and moved to another, which he also lost. Eventually he got tenure at a university in London, which is where he's still working. Or was until..." she sighed and looked down briefly.

"Anyway, I had hoped with the increase in salary a university position would give him, it would help our marriage. Finances were always a huge strain. It was the main reason I started working at the paper myself. He got me a job at his old firm. He had a few contacts who were still speaking to him at that time. It was the same paper who took over The Plumpton Mallet Gazette. But, if you don't adjust your lifestyle, and Monty always lived way above his means, then problems with money will always be there. When the paper decided to take over here, I jumped at the chance to move in order to get away from him. He was furious, as you can imagine, and I spent many of my first months here in an almost permanent state of terror that he'd turn up and drag me back. But he never did, which surprised me. I realise now he was just biding his time and deliberately making sure I was living in fear of his coming after me. I was just beginning to relax a little and was sure he'd finished with me when he accused me of stealing from him. I took my share of our savings out of the joint bank account, as you know. It was every bit my money as his, but of course he didn't see that. I suppose I should have just left it where it was and cut my losses."

"You did the right thing, Abigail. Like you said, that money was yours too, and you'd earned it fair and square. It was a brave thing to do."

"I do remember Monty being very good at making enemies, especially out of friends. Take Tom, for instance. The two of them were as thick as thieves for the longest time. Now Tom can't stand the sight of him."

"Do you think it was Tom who killed him?" Lilly asked.

"He certainly had enough motive, but I thought he was in custody at the time?"

Lilly shook her head. "No, according to Bonnie he'd already been released, but she said it wasn't possible time wise for Tom to have killed him."

"Why is Bonnie so sure it was James?" Abigail asked.

"Honestly? I don't think she is sure, but what scant evidence there is seems to point to him," Lilly said, then went on to explain Bonnie's reasons.

"Well, of course James' fingerprints were on the mug," Abigail said in exasperation. "He helped me sort them all out the morning of the market, before we delivered them to the various locations. Monty could have got that mug from anywhere."

"I didn't realise James had done that with you?"

"Yes, he helped me open up all the packaging before the event even started. His prints are probably on at least half of them because we checked the printing quality at the same time."

"And I still can't fathom where James was supposed to have got the cyanide from," Lilly said. "I'm glad we're on the same page about this, Abigail."

"Oh, absolutely we are," Abigail said indignantly. "Bonnie has definitely got it wrong this time."

"I appreciate you talking it through with me. I think I'll go to the police station and see if Bonnie will let me talk to James. We need to ascertain his alibi and I can also let him know Stacey has contacted his solicitor if he doesn't know already."

"Okay. Will you let me know how it goes and send my best wishes to James? Tell him to hang in there from me. We'll get it all sorted out."

"Of course. Bye, Abigail. And well done with the tea room, it looks fantastic."

※

EVEN THOUGH THE walk to the police station wasn't far, it was made twice as long due to the amount of snow that had fallen. Lilly found herself trudging through crunchy snow a foot deep, but luckily the blizzard had died down and only a few gentle flakes were now falling. By the time she arrived, her teeth were chattering and she could no longer feel her toes and fingers.

She stamped the snow from her boots at the door, then approached the reception desk. The constable on duty slid open the Perspex window, and she asked to see Bonnie. She was told to wait while he passed on the message, so with no one else around, Lilly chose the seat nearest the radiator. A few minutes later, Bonnie came through to the waiting area.

"What can I do for you, Lilly?"

"I want to visit James, Bonnie. Is that all right?"

Bonnie shook her head. "I'm sorry, Lilly, but I'm afraid it's not. I've just finished talking with him and..."

"Finished being the operative word? Please, Bonnie. I know deep down you don't think he murdered Monty. And I've just spoken with Abigail, who told me James helped her unpack the take out mugs before the market, so his fingerprints are likely to be on a lot of them for that reason." Bonnie raised an eyebrow at this additional bit of news, but said nothing. "Let me talk to him and see what I can find out. I expect Stacey has got hold of his solicitor by now, anyway. He's probably on his way. You'll not get much more out of him then."

Bonnie rolled her eyes. "Fine, but you can't stay long and just so you know, I will be listening in. I'll put you both in the interview room."

"Thanks, Bonnie."

Lilly was led through to the back part of the station via a door from the waiting room. Down a long corridor and into a bland, bare room consisting of a battered table with a grey, worn Formica top and a single chair either side. She sat down and waited for James to arrive while listening to the loud Tick-Tock of a large analog clock positioned high on the side wall. Apart from an old fashioned radiator clunking away noisily in an attempt to heat the place, it was the only other item in the room.

A moment later, James was escorted in by a constable who remained in the room but took an unobtrusive position against the wall.

"Lilly! Oh, what a relief to see you," James said, hurriedly taking the seat opposite hers. "Is Stacey all right?"

"She's fine. She was upset, obviously, but more out of anger on your behalf, I think. Honestly, she's handling it very well, James, so try not to worry about her. I expect she's already made the call you asked her to by now."

He exhaled. "That's my daughter," he said in a proud voice. "But you're sure she's all right?"

Lilly nodded. "But what about you, James? How are you?"

"Rattled, to be honest. And more than a bit angry. I obviously didn't kill Monty, but it doesn't look very good, does it? My fingerprints being on the poisoned cup, although they'll probably be on most of them considering I helped Abigail unpack the blasted things. Then there's the history I have with the man."

"Yes, speaking of your history, can you tell me what happened? I understand there was some sort of physical fight between you?"

He ran his fingers through his greying hair, causing it to stick up in all directions, and leaned back with a sigh. "Yes, there was, much to my shame. And forgive me if I sound like a petulant schoolboy, but it wasn't me who started it. He was apoplectic that I'd gone to the board and reported what I'd heard from his female students, and threatened to give me a good pounding. He would have done so there and then had I not told him, in less polite terms, to get lost. In hindsight I should have just kept my big mouth shut, but I couldn't resist telling him that if he laid so much as a finger on me I'd report that to the board too."

"I imagine that didn't go down too well?" Lilly said.

"And you'd be correct. It escalated things, and we ended up in a heated slanging match, with me telling him what the students had shared with me and how disgusted I was with him. I told him in no uncertain terms that he wasn't fit to be a teacher and should be dismissed immediately. Of course, he became even more aggressive then and demanded I tell him their names. Well, I certainly wasn't going to divulge that information and put the girls at risk. It had taken a lot of courage to tell me what they did." He sighed and leaned forward, putting his arms on the table. "To be honest, Lilly, I didn't truly understand what the man was capable of. I had never seen him so riled. We'd not worked closely in the past, as I told you before, but he was definitely a Jekyll and Hyde character. With more emphasis on Edward Hyde, unfortunately."

"Then what happened?" Lilly asked. She was relieved James hadn't given Monty the names of his accusers. Doing so would have put them in danger. It was a sign of both morality and professionalism in James' favour as far as she was concerned. With principles like that, how could he possibly then have gone on to commit murder?

"He shoved me. I didn't retaliate, just shouted at him to get out of my office. He shoved me a second time, straight into my desk, and nearly knocked over an object I held dear. He saw me check it was safe and deduced it was something I cared about. He snatched it off my desk and when I warned him to put it down, he threw it against the wall where it shattered."

"What was it?" Lilly hadn't pegged James as being the sentimental type particularly, and wondered what could have elicited such a response.

"It was a glass paperweight that my mother gave me as a congratulatory gift when I first took tenure at the university. She died shortly after. I was furious. He was just being vindictive."

"I'm sorry. What did you do?"

"I shoved him back, of course. He'd already assaulted me twice and deliberately broken the paperweight, which he knew meant a lot to me. It was the final straw. I shouldn't have done it. I was just trying to get him out of my office. Anyway, he got me in a headlock and before I knew it, we'd stumbled out into the corridor and were brawling in view of half the students. I think that was the main issue actually, that the students witnessed the whole sorry affair. One of my colleagues dragged Monty off me, then of course the board had to get involved. We were both up for tenure and were extremely lucky we didn't lose our jobs on the back of it. The investigation into Monty's behaviour with the female students was still ongoing at that time as well."

"When did this happen, James?"

"The fight was last year," he replied. "Eventually, it was concluded with neither of us being punished, but we were severely reprimanded and were warned we'd be out on our ears if it happened again. Nothing less than I would expect. It was very unprofessional. I break out in a cold sweat every time I think about it. Although I was told later by a colleague that the board realised Monty had been the instigator and that I was simply defending myself. He had a reputation as a troublemaker by that time, you see. As far as the sexual harassment is concerned, that's still being investigated as far as I'm aware. Although, now he's dead, I expect that will end."

"How had things been between the two of you since the fight? It must have been a difficult environment to work in?" Lilly said.

"I simply avoided him. I certainly didn't want a repeat of what had happened, so the best way to ensure it was to stay out of his way. I'm pleased to say it worked. He bad mouths me at every opportunity, of course, or he did, rather, but no one believes a word he says. As far as I'm concerned, I've put it all behind me. I'm still annoyed about my mother's gift, but there's nothing I can do about it. There are more important things in my life now, my daughter for one. There's nothing I would do to jeopardise our relationship, Lilly. As much as I disliked Monty, I certainly didn't kill him. And quite frankly, I'm shocked and hurt anyone would think I had."

"I believe you, James." Lilly replied. "I'm sure you'll be hearing from Stacey shortly. For now, sit tight. We are going to get this misunderstanding sorted out."

James sighed. "Thank you, Lilly."

Chapter Ten

LILLY WAS ESCORTED back to the waiting room and decided to stay until she could speak to Bonnie again. She was still wondering about Tom Livingstone. He had more than enough reason to kill Monty. His former friend had cost him his job, his reputation, and his career. And probably several friends in the process. There was no way he would ever get another job as a police officer, no matter whereabouts in the country he applied. Unquestionably, Tom also had anger issues, proved by the way he had attacked Monty on market day. But just how angry was he? Enough to kill Monty? Lilly thought it was more than possible. He was certainly a better suspect than James.

She recalled Bonnie telling her that Tom had been released too late to have poisoned Monty, but did Bonnie know that for a fact, or had she just been informed by one of the other police officers and taken it at face value? Now she came to think about it a bit more, Bonnie hadn't come across as being absolutely sure when she'd told her. Had she double-checked the time Tom had been let out? It was one of the questions she needed to ask her. If Lilly could prove Tom had had enough time to poison Monty, then it could very well let James off the hook. Or at the very least, get him out of jail while investigations were ongoing. She really needed to do some investigating herself. She knew her detective friend might not like it, but she was convinced Bonnie would come round to her way of thinking if only she could find the right evidence.

She was still hugging the radiator and mulling over her next step when Bonnie came into the reception. Lilly asked her if she knew without a shadow of a doubt that Tom had been released too late to have poisoned Monty?

"That's what I was told, Lilly. I was back at the market at the time, as you know, but I promise I will double check if it sets your mind at ease. And for what it's worth, I don't really think James is our culprit. Unfortunately, what I believe and the evidence in front of me are completely opposite, and I can only do my job based on the current evidence."

Lilly nodded. It made her feel a bit better that Bonnie didn't really believe James was guilty and would check when Tom was released. That's all she could hope for at the moment. Bonnie was called over by the desk sergeant, who handed her a file. After reviewing the contents briefly, she closed it and looked over Lilly's shoulder. "Laura, I have that police report for you."

Lilly turned and found Laura Smith had been sitting unobtrusively in a corner of the waiting room. She stood up and took the file. "That's great. Thank you, Bonnie."

"Laura," Lilly said. "I'm so sorry, I didn't realise you were there. You should have said something. How are you?"

"Just getting on with it, I suppose," she said, her eyes bleak. "What more can I do?"

"I need to get back to work," Bonnie said. "Good luck, Laura. I'll be in touch, Lilly."

"What's going on?" Lilly asked Laura once Bonnie had gone. The poor woman looked exhausted and unkempt, with dark circles beneath her eyes. Most unlike the Laura she knew.

"I need the report for the insurance company. But I'm not sure now that they'll pay out and if they don't, I'll be ruined. I'm worried sick I'm going to be in debt. I'm contemplating suing both Tom and Monty for damages. You know, part of me is glad that Monty person is dead," she said, on the verge of tears.

"Oh, Laura," Lilly said, putting her arm around the woman's shoulder. "I don't believe you mean that."

Lilly knew Laura quite well, and she'd never heard her speak this way before. For a fleeting moment, it crossed Lilly's mind that Laura might have had something to do with Monty's death. If the insurance company was refusing to pay out, Laura would not only lose her business but be in a mountain of debt. That in itself was a strong motive. People had killed for far less. But was Laura really capable of murder? And on the day itself, had she actually had the time to do it? She obviously wouldn't have known about the issues with the insurance money on the day of the market, but perhaps her anger had been fueled by the loss of all her hard work?

"Sorry," Laura said. "That sounded terrible, didn't it? You're right, I didn't mean it. It's just been a really rough couple of days."

Lilly's heart went out to Laura. Sometimes all you needed was a sympathetic ear. Perhaps being able to talk out her problems with someone over a drink and meal would help put things in perspective. *Plus*, Lilly thought, *I might learn something which will shed more light on the murder.* Not just for James' sake, but for Stacey's as well, she wanted him free and back among family and friends as soon as possible.

"Come on, Laura, let's go and get a drink and a bite to eat. There's a pub not far we can walk to. I'd like to help if I can."

"You don't have to do that, Lilly."

"I know, but I want to. Come on, I'm not taking no for an answer."

She guided a weary Laura out of the station and despite her protestations, Laura didn't object.

MOST OF THE pubs in Plumpton Mallet were old buildings dating back hundreds of years, and the Dog and Duck was no exception. From the street you descended a couple of old stone steps, worn to a dip in the centre from years of footfall, and being careful not to bang your head on the lintel entered a small snug with the bar across the back, a stone flagged floor and a fire roaring in the hearth where two Christmas Stockings were hanging from the sides of the mantelpiece. They took a table near the mullion window and settled down to read the menu. Once they'd chosen, Lilly went to the bar to order and pay.

The pub was already well into the Christmas spirit with cheery festive songs playing through the numerous speakers, which Lilly found herself humming along to. On the end of the bar was a small silver Christmas tree with fibre optic lights continually changing from deep magenta all the way through to pale gold. In the corner of the snug where she was standing, a large, realistic Douglas fir was a fully dressed vision with sparkling warm fairy lights and adorned with crackers and baubles in red, green and gold and smothered with long garlands of silver tinsel. Abigail would love it, Lilly thought.

While she waited for their wine, she poked her head through the archway into the next room and found another tree, this time an artificial white pine covered in sparkling silvery snow, pine cones and red and green led lights.

She moved back to the bar, thanked the barman for the drinks and took them back to the table where Laura was waiting.

"It's so nice here," Laura said, visibly beginning to relax.

"Have you not been before?"

"Once, a long time ago, but I don't think it was called the Dog and Duck then?"

"It used to be called The Pheasant."

"Yes, that's it. The inside hasn't changed much, though. And it's lovely and warm."

They made small talk for a while until their food arrived and then Lilly asked about the report Laura had obtained from Bonnie.

"You mentioned legal action against Monty and Tom?"

"Oh, Lilly, I wouldn't normally consider it, but it's all gone wrong. I put a claim into my insurance company but they've said they won't cover the damages."

"What? Why on earth would they say that? I know they're sticklers for the fine detail, but surely your claim is valid? It was accidental damage caused by a fight."

"There was a brief lapse in my coverage. My original company was putting up my premiums by a lot, so I decided to shop around and see if I could find a cheaper alternative. I found one on-line and immediately called them. I am almost positive I started it before my other cover lapsed, but they're now saying it started three days after my former policy ran out. Apparently, there's something in the fine print I must have missed. So there were three days I wasn't insured by anyone, and with the worst luck possible, one of those was the day of the Christmas Market. Now neither of them will help me. I'm stuck without a way to pay for everything that got damaged or the loans I took to make them all in the first place."

"Oh, Laura, I am so sorry. Were you able to salvage anything at all from the breakages?"

Laura shook her head. "Very little. Much of it had too many impurities mixed in with it. There are hours and hours of work just gone and I hadn't even had a chance to make many sales before everything was broken."

"I assume you've spoken with a solicitor about trying to get something from Tom and from Monty's estate?"

"Yes, and he cost a pretty penny, too. But my only chance to get anything is through Monty's estate. Tom, it turns out, has practically nothing."

"I'm surprised to hear Monty had anything. From what I understand, he was terrible with money and lived way beyond his means."

"Apparently he had a trust or something from his father, which he's never touched for some reason. Maybe there was some sort of clause preventing it, I don't know. But if I can get a percentage of that, it should at least cover some of my losses. I doubt it will be much, though. I don't know what to do, Lilly. I've worked so hard to get to the point where I had a profitable business, now a stupid lapse in insurance cover combined with two brainless men who decided to have a brawl in the street, and everything's ruined."

Lilly sighed. No amount of comfort food or chatting with friends was going to fix this. All she could do was to be there for Laura if she was needed. Though it did make her realise how many enemies Monty had made. Abigail, James, Tom, now Laura. And she suspected these were only the tip of the iceberg when it came to people who held a grudge against him. Maybe she should try and talk to Tom next?

As they ate, Lilly thought about Tom and wondered where he was. She couldn't remember him saying he was staying in Plumpton Mallet. He could easily have returned home now he no longer had a job interview to go to. She hoped Bonnie had told him to stay close before they'd let him out of jail.

Once they'd finished eating, Laura thanked Lilly for lending her a shoulder and Lilly elicited a promise from her, that if there was anything she could do to help, she must tell her. Once Laura had left, Lilly stayed in the warmth of the pub and took out her phone. There was one person she really wanted to talk things through with. Archie. He should be back from his cousin's house now and, knowing her investigative reporter friend, he would more than likely know the whereabouts of Tom Livingstone.

"MY FAVOURITE TEASHOP owner," he said, as bright as ever when he answered her call. "To what do I owe the pleasure?"

"And just how many tea shop owners do you know, Archie Brown?"

"Yes, you've got me there, Miss Tweed. But you're utterly unique. There could only be one of you."

Lilly laughed. "How was your family visit?"

"Actually, it was very nice indeed. I'm just on my way back now, as a matter of fact. I stayed longer than I intended. You'll no doubt be pleased to know that the tea set was highly approved of and was safely hidden in the garden shed. The only place 'her indoors' is not allowed to venture so the Christmas surprise will not be spoiled. I hear there's been quite a lot happening in my short absence."

"You've spoken to Bonnie then?"

"I have. I must say I'm surprised she has arrested James."

"She says she has to go by the evidence in front of her, not by her personal feelings. She doesn't really think he did it. Although I'll admit I'm more than a little annoyed with her at the moment."

"So, what do you need, Lilly? I assume you've decided to investigate yourself?"

A Frosty Combination

"You know me, Archie. I don't know how to mind my own business. Especially when an innocent friend is involved. I was wondering if you happened to know what happened to Tom Livingstone?"

"I do. He was taken straight to the hospital by the constable after the fight at the market. He'd been badly cut and needed medical attention. The police obviously couldn't risk anything happening to him if he was thrown into a cell without seeing a doctor. He's due to go back for a follow up today. Actually, what time is it? Yes, he's probably there now."

"How on earth do you know this, Archie?"

"I have an orderly friend at the hospital. But, here's the thing, Lilly, Tom never even set foot in the police station."

"What? But I thought he was arrested?"

"I'm afraid not. I spoke to a very angry Bonnie earlier. The constable let him off with a warning rather than book him. She told me you were there to visit James and asked her to double check when Tom was released. She did, and this is what she found out."

"I bet the constable is regretting that decision now," Lilly said.

"Indeed. Bonnie's on the warpath. If it turns out Tom did kill Monty, then Bonnie will have his job. His excuse was he thought Tom had learned his lesson after his injury in the fight and his need for a hospital visit. It sounds as though Tom sweet-talked him a bit. You know, former police officer, one of the lads, and all that guff. Reading between the lines, I also think this particular constable has a bit of an issue taking orders from a woman."

"Bonnie must have her sights set on Tom now, then?"

"She has. Depending on when Tom left for the hospital on the day of the murder, he could very well have had the opportunity to kill Monty."

"You said Tom is at the hospital now?"

"That's right."

"I appreciate the tip, Archie."

"Anytime. Just share what you know with me, will you?"

"Of course. You're my favourite Investigative Journalist, Mr Brown."

Archie laughed. "Touché, Miss Tweed. Touché."

RELUCTANTLY LEAVING THE warmth of the Dog and Duck and venturing into the chilly temperature outside, Lilly trudged slowly back to the town car-park. The snow had been falling continuously while she'd been chatting with Archie and was now several inches deeper. By the time she got to the car, her coat was covered in a layer of white. She put the heater on full blast while she scraped the new snowfall off all the windows, then inside stripped off her wet gloves and scarf, and sent a quick text to Rodney apologising for not being back in time and leaving him to lock up the shop. She got a quick reply saying it was no problem, as Stacey had helped. Earl was also with her in the flat, so would be perfectly happy until she got back.

Even though the council gritters had been out and done the main roads, it was still a slow journey to the hospital, as visibility was poor and every car on the road had slowed to a crawl. She had her windscreen wipers on full blast, but

A Frosty Combination

they seemed to make little difference. She'd been hoping that when she'd called him, Archie would already have been back in Plumpton Mallet, as she would have loved some company. If she found Tom at the hospital, she wasn't sure what his reaction would be, and it would have been nice to have some support. But never mind, she'd just have to deal with it herself and hope she wouldn't make him angry with her questions.

Eventually, half an hour longer than it would normally have taken, Lilly parked the car across from the hospital entrance and walked over. She waited behind two people at the reception desk, then, when it was her turn, asked if Tom Livingstone was still there.

"Are you a relative?"

Lilly shook her head. "No. A friend," she said. A little white lie, but it couldn't be helped. "I'm supposed to be giving him a lift home, but I'm a bit late and hoping he hasn't left already."

The receptionist tapped on a computer screen then informed her he was still in the building, but should be finished with his appointment very soon if she'd like to take a seat in the waiting area. Lilly thanked her, but rather than wait where Tom could see her, she decided to peruse the hospital gift shop. It still gave her a good view of the reception area and the exit without being too obvious.

Walking around the shop, she spied a leather key fob with the image of an American Bald Eagle. It gave her an idea. James was an avid American history buff and knew all sorts of quirky information. He'd actually been instrumental in helping her solve a previous case at a local book club demonstration because of his arcane knowledge. She decided to put together a gift basket filled with Americana. She envisioned a red, white, and blue hamper filled with trinkets and books. After buying the key fob, she left the shop and caught sight of Tom approaching the reception desk.

"Tom," she called out. He spun round, surprised at first, then scowled when he realised who it was.

"What do you want?"

She could see his face was badly cut and bruised. He had a bandage on the side of his neck and a row of stitches across his left eyebrow. She'd seen the blood on him the day of the fight but hadn't realised he'd been as badly hurt as he had.

"Ouch," she said in sympathy.

He rolled his eyes and began to walk away. She scurried after him, catching up at the reception desk.

"I'm sorry. I was surprised when you turned around. I hadn't realised how bad your injuries were."

"Yeah, well, that's Monty for you. Never knows when to stop. He decided to smash one of the glass ornaments in my face when we were fighting. That did most of the damage."

"So how are you?" she asked. She could tell he wanted to leave, but was waiting for some paperwork from the nurse.

"Would you please leave me alone?" he snapped. "I don't want to talk to you or anyone else about what happened."

Lilly frowned but said nothing, watching as he filled in and signed the paperwork the nurse handed him. She raised a brow and promptly reached into her pocket, pulling out a letter. She'd recognised his handwriting. "I got your letter, Tom," she said.

He slid the paperwork back to the nurse, took his copy, and faced Lilly.

"What are you talking about?"

She took his arm and gently guided him away from the desk. "I'm the tea shop agony aunt. Don't you remember you asked on market day why the café had that name, and me and Abigail said it was us? I wrote back to you but haven't had a chance to post it yet. It's still in my pocket along with the letter you wrote."

He looked embarrassed. "Please lower your voice. I thought they were supposed to be anonymous? I specifically took a box at the Plumpton Mallet post office, so it would be! I wrote and posted that letter before I even got to your stall and by the time I realised who you were it was too late. I couldn't retrieve it. I was hoping you'd just post the reply and I could leave without you knowing it was me."

"Most people address me by name when they write. I should have realised your letter wasn't from a local. But, as I haven't posted it yet and we're both here, I could answer you in person if you're willing?"

He paused for a while, and then shrugged in resignation. "Fine," he said. "It makes no odds now you know it was me that wrote it."

They moved to a couple of hard plastic seats in a private corner, next to several empty wheel chairs waiting for porters to move patients to their appointments, and a weighing machine. Lilly read the letter.

"Dear Agony Aunt," she began. "I have acquired an unfortunate reputation that is affecting both my personal and professional life. I'm worried I will never be able to escape this. I have made mistakes in my life, but I want to do better. How can I show people I have changed, particularly in professional settings?"

"Yes, that's mine," Tom said. Blushing furiously.

Lilly nodded. "My first question obviously is, have you changed, Tom?"

"Look, if I'd realised you were the agony aunt, I wouldn't have written in. You're not exactly impartial, are you? I know you are friends and business partners with Abigail."

"You're right, I am. But I'm always impartial when it comes to writing advice, Tom. I'd make a poor agony aunt if I wasn't. Besides, when I answered your letter, I didn't know it was from you. Knowing you helped Monty cover up his abuse doesn't paint you in a very good light, but the fact you bothered to write and ask for help speaks volumes. It makes me think you really do want to change even if you haven't started yet. It's the first step. I have to ask though, did you kill Monty?"

"Of course not. But I'm not sorry he's dead." He sighed deeply. "What you've got to understand is that Monty and me were good friends, at least I thought we were. Looking back, I can see Monty didn't know how to have friends, or be one. But at the time, I supported him and covered up what he was doing because I couldn't believe my friend was that sort of man. I honestly thought at the time he and Abigail could work it out. It was the wrong thing to do. I realise that now. He was putting her through sheer hell and I didn't believe it."

"So, what happened in London exactly? I know you were looking for work in Plumpton Mallet."

He shrugged. "Word got around about what was happening with Monty and Abigail and how I covered up for him. He'd started knocking around some other woman he was having a bit of a fling with. I covered that up too."

Lilly gasped. She couldn't help herself.

"Yeah. I'm more ashamed than you'll ever know. I was found out and lost my job. When I told Monty, he laughed and said I could always become a nightclub bouncer or a security guard. Just proves we were never really friends, doesn't it? I regret ever meeting him. I should have done something about his behaviour but I didn't and now it's ruined my life."

"My advice is that you need a career change, Tom," Lilly said.

"What? But I'm a copper."

"No, Tom. You're not. Not anymore, and considering how you handled Monty's conduct, I'd question whether you were fit for the position in the first place."

"Now wait just a minute!" Tom began, but Lilly interrupted.

"You asked for my advice and I'm giving it to you. You might not like it. The truth is difficult to hear sometimes, but you know it is the truth. I think you should seriously consider getting some form of counselling. You know what you did was wrong, but you need to understand why you made the decisions you did. You covered up for and defended a man who was abusing his wife behind closed doors. I think it's time you asked yourself why. I also think you should apply to be a volunteer at a woman's shelter and see first-hand what horrendous damage men like Monty inflict on women. It will give you a better perspective."

Tom stared at her for so long she began to feel a little uncomfortable. "What is it?"

"Sorry, I was thinking. It's good advice you've given me. I suppose I never really expected it from an agony aunt. I thought it would be some sort of naff response like you see in the national papers."

"We're not all the same, Tom. The question now is whether you choose to take it? You have a chance to turn your life around and start putting something positive and good back into the world. I really hope you do. And one other bit of advice, let go of the anger. You'll never be able to move forward unless you do. You may think Monty ruined your life, but he wasn't able to do it without your consent and cooperation, and he's now paid the ultimate price, wouldn't you say? You have a chance to make your life and those around you much better. To make amends. He'll never be able to do that now, his time is over." She stood up. "Good luck, Tom," she said, and walked away.

As she drove home, she ran through the conversation. She was almost sure Tom hadn't murdered Monty, and she admitted to herself that while she didn't really like the man very much, he had seemed genuinely ashamed of his past behaviour and was carrying more than a little guilt. She felt he deserved a second chance. She only hoped he had been as honest as he'd appeared to be and hadn't managed to pull the wool over her eyes.

Chapter Eleven

THE NEXT MORNING, Lilly was almost at the front door when the cottage telephone rang. She dashed back down the hall to answer it and saw it was the shop number. Immediately her heart began to pound. Surely this early in the morning it could only mean something was wrong? She snatched up the receiver.

"Hello, Stacey? What's wrong?"

"Surprise!" it was James' voice.

"James!" she said. She could hear a happy Stacey in the background, along with Rodney, both of them laughing. "Oh, my goodness, you're out!"

"Yes. Isn't it marvellous? Sorry if I caused you a bit of a panic just then, Stacey convinced me to call from the shop phone."

"No, it's fine. I'm just relieved. When did you get out?"

"Last night. I should have called then, but Stacey and I went out for dinner to celebrate and lost track of time."

"Don't be silly. There was no need to call me. So, what was it that changed Bonnie's mind?"

"Actually, I think I have Rodney to thank for that. Once he realised I was being blamed for killing Monty and held at the police station, he went to speak to her and insisted she test for fingerprint samples on a cross section of other take out cups. Apparently, she took several from the waste bins at the both the café and the tea shop, some unused from both places and those still in the store. It was a good assortment. And guess what? My fingerprints were on all of them. Obviously she told me not to leave Plumpton Mallet, but I wasn't going to, anyway. I've not been fully cleared as it were, but at least I'm not languishing in a cell during the run up to Christmas. There's only ten days left and I've hardly started on my shopping. Stacey and I will have to forgo our trip to London, of course, but we are both perfectly fine with that. The main thing is we'll be able to spend it together."

"I am so glad to hear you're out, James. You have no idea what a relief it is for me," she said. Although privately she thought this was something Bonnie should have done right at the beginning rather than subject James to time in a cell. Not to mention worrying Stacey, and everyone else.

"For me as well, Lilly. It was an anxious time, but now I'm sitting back in the shop, drinking some lovely Lavender tea which Rodney has just brewed, with my daughter and determined to forget all about it."

"Lavender is a very good choice. Save me some, will you? I'll be there shortly."

A Frosty Combination

T HE ROAD WAS once again lethal with black ice as she carefully drove to the shop. Made all the more perilous by the sudden gusts of wind which threatened to bowl her small car off the road. She gripped tightly to the steering wheel, concentrating hard, and was relieved to finally make it to the car park without incident.

Inside, she was greeted by a very happy Stacey, Rodney and James, who were all drinking tea before the shop was due to open. After saying good morning to Earl in the window, she joined the others at the counter.

"What does it feel like to be a free man then, James?" she asked with a grin.

"A blessed relief. But I'm still a bit worried if I'm honest. Bonnie said the presence of my fingerprints alone wasn't enough to convict me now, but I wasn't to get too comfortable. It looks as though I'm still a main suspect and as such feel as though I have a black cloud hanging over my head. Until the real perpetrator is caught, I don't think I'll be able to relax. But I'm at a loss as to how to convince her I had nothing to do with Monty's death."

"I don't think you can, dad," Stacey said. "She's got to find the evidence that points to someone else and clears you. But, if it helps, I do trust her to do her job properly, especially as she's found loads of other prints on the cups. She'll be extra cautious now, don't you think?"

Lilly nodded. "I agree with Stacey. We need to let Bonnie continue with her investigation, but that's not to say we can't do a bit of sleuthing ourselves."

"Right," Rodney said. "Hopefully, Bonnie will find what she needs to absolve you, James. But I have to say whoever did get rid of him, did the world a favour."

"Rodney!" Lilly exclaimed.

"I know, I know," he replied. "Maybe that was a bit much, but let's be realistic. He beat up and terrorised his wife for years and made her whole life miserable. Then he followed her here and threatened her. He tried to pick a fight with me. He attacked James. He had a street brawl with Tom and ruined Laura's stall, and was responsible for Tom ending up in hospital. And there's probably more we don't know about. He was a really nasty piece of work."

Lilly sighed. "Yes, that's all true, although some of that was Tom's fault. He started the fight that ruined all Laura's hard work."

"Yeah, but Monty was responsible for him losing his job. He'd obviously had enough. Personally, I can't blame the man for wanting to give Monty wallop. But, I really feel sorry for poor Laura," Rodney said. "Has anyone heard from her since?"

"I bumped into her last evening. I took her for an early dinner. Things aren't looking good for her business at the moment," Lilly said.

"You know, I'm almost finished developing the photos I took on the day. I took quite a few of her stall before the fight happened. Do you think she'd like them?"

"I do, Rodney," Lilly said. "It's a good idea, actually. She might be able to use them for promotion. She's worried she'll have to give up her glass making business altogether and get a job."

"How dreadful for her," James said with a sad shake of his head.

"I think I'll go back and see Bonnie later," Lilly said. "After the morning rush is over. See if she is prepared to update me on the investigation."

"Do you think she will?" James asked. "With you and I being friends, I mean? She might see it as too much of a conflict."

Lilly smiled, surprisingly glad that James considered them friends considering their shaky start. She found she agreed with him. "Yes, that's more than possible. Considering how close we all are. Not only to the case, but to one another. It's put her in a difficult position. She might appreciate my help, or she'll want to keep us all at arm's length. But I won't know until I ask."

Lilly hoped Bonnie would welcome her assistance and be willing to share what she'd uncovered to date. She was eager to know if there had been any additional evidence found that would exonerate James. Privately, she thought it must be someone from out of town who'd murdered Monty. Somebody from his past who he'd damaged in some way and who had followed him to Plumpton Mallet to get their own back. She just couldn't countenance it being one of her friends.

The first customer of the day arrived, and Rodney went to help. She wanted several boxes of the Christmas peppermint and cranberry blend. Lilly also noticed they were running low on chamomile, lavender, orange and Echinacea, so Stacey went to the store room to bring back additional stock.

"We thought these might start to sell," Stacey said to Lilly. "So dad and me made up a bunch of bags. Our customers are trying to thwart the dreaded colds."

"Very good choices, Stacey. All those alone, or a tailored blend, will help them get over the bug faster and with fewer symptoms."

Stacey nodded. "Yep, that's what Rodney's been telling everyone."

Lilly was glad Rodney was learning about the medicinal quality of her teas, although his knowledge was already very good to begin with. Especially for someone under the age of thirty. In this weather, people were bound to start having sniffles, so she suggested brewing the orange spice for samples and promote it as the Tea of the Day. She told Rodney, and he changed the special board, putting it in the window.

Stacey and James started to replenish the shelves, where numerous sales had resulted in spaces, laughing as they did so. Lilly noticed Stacey hardly let her father out of her sight. She was pleased they were reunited, and determined there wouldn't be another separation.

She helped another couple of customers while Rodney sold a Christmas tea set and a set of Irish linen napkins with holly embroidered in the corners.

Mid morning the customers began to dwindle and with three staff in place, Lilly felt it was a good time to go and see Bonnie. She filled a take away mug with the orange spice blend. It would keep her warm while she walked to the station.

A Frosty Combination

THE SNOW MADE a satisfying crunch under her boots as she made her way across the market square to the police station, but it was still bitterly cold and she was glad she'd had the foresight to bring a steaming hot cup of tea with her.

Once again, she entered the station and approached the reception desk. Giving her name and the reason for her visit, she then sat and waited for Bonnie. A moment later, a constable came and collected her.

"She's on the phone at the moment but said you could wait in her office while she finished."

The constable knocked on the door and opened it. Bonnie waved her in and indicated she should take a seat until she was free to talk.

"All right, thanks," Bonnie said. "Yes, email it to me straight away. Okay, thanks," she said, ending the call and with a heartfelt sigh, turned to Lilly. "The mortuary. I should have the pathology report from Dr Perry imminently."

"That's good news, isn't it? Hopefully, there's something there you can use to build the case?"

Bonnie shook her head. "There isn't. I've already had the salient information from him verbally. Apart from the poison, which we know to be cyanide or a derivative of, the only other thing of note was extreme cirrhosis of the liver. From a lifetime of drinking, apparently. He certainly wasn't going to reach old age, that's for sure."

Lilly nodded, unsurprised. "Well, at least James is out now. I understand Rodney came to see you?"

Bonnie sat back in her chair and rolled her eyes. "He did. He sat where you are now and told me what he thought

I should be doing. As if I'd been born yesterday and couldn't think for myself. I'd already started doing what he suggested on the back of what you'd already told me, and if he hadn't been so polite about it, I'd have probably snapped his head off. As it was, I told him what a great idea he'd come up with, thanked him from coming in and showed him out."

Lilly laughed. "He was supporting a friend. He knows as well as we all do that James didn't kill Monty."

"He's not off the hook yet, Lilly," Bonnie said seriously.

"Oh, Bonnie," Lilly groaned. "James is innocent."

"Well, he's still my main suspect. And unless we find the proverbial smoking gun, he's going to remain that way."

"Right," Lilly said, standing up and removing her coat. "Let's find it then. What about Monty's past? Have you checked that? We've been concentrating on the locals and the likes of Tom, who was here on market day, but there was a massive influx of tourists here for the event. Maybe there was someone here we didn't know about? Someone with a grudge who followed him to Plumpton Mallet and saw an opportunity? It's apparent he left numerous destroyed lives in his wake."

"Maybe?" Bonnie said, but she sounded dubious.

Lilly checked her watch. "It's almost lunchtime. Why don't I sort that out while you make some calls, or whatever it is you need to do? We can go through what you find out together?"

"I've never known anyone as annoyingly persistent as you, Lilly Tweed."

"Why don't you just admit it, Bonnie? You want my help."

Bonnie chuckled. "Fine, Miss Marple, just make sure you get extra cheese on my pizza," she said, reaching for the phone and pressing an extension number to one of the desks in the back office.

WHILE BONNIE GOT to work, Lilly telephoned the local pizza shop and placed her order, only to be told that due to the copious amount of orders combined with the atrocious weather and the dangerous state of the roads, delivery would be around an hour. Alternatively, it would be ready to collect in fifteen minutes. With the pizza parlour only being at the other side of the car park, it would take around ten minutes walk each way, so she informed Bonnie she'd be back in half an hour and set off.

It was a brisk walk each way in the freezing cold and naturally, the food was cold when she got back. She heated the pizzas in the microwave at the police station and was taking them back to Bonnie's office when she saw a young female constable carrying a stack of files. She was headed in the same direction. Lilly hurried after her and they entered Bonnie's office together.

"I've got those files you wanted," she said to Bonnie.

Bonnie looked up, the smile on her face replaced by shock at the size of the stack.

"All those are part of Montgomery Douglas's criminal record?"

The young woman blinked. "Who?"

"The records I asked you to get? I can't believe they got here so quickly, especially considering how many there are. They must have sent a courier," Bonnie said, eyeing the teetering pile on her desk in dismay. "How come they're all in old card files? Did you do that after they'd been sent?"

"Sent?" The young policewoman looked horribly confused, and it was increasingly clear she had misunderstood Bonnie's request.

"Montgomery Douglas," Bonnie said, becoming slightly annoyed. "The murder we are investigating, Jennifer. I thought they would have e-mailed them for you to print off. I never expected hard copies."

"I'm so sorry, Bonnie, I got the wrong end of the stick."

Bonnie sighed. "What did you do?"

"When you phoned through, I was on the other line with an irate woman whose drunken husband hadn't come back from the pub last night. She was giving me earache and demanding I go out and find him. I was distracted and wrote down domestic abuse cases. When I came off the phone, I got the records of the Plumpton Mallet cases."

"How far did you go back?" Bonnie said, frowning.

"Well, all of them," Jennifer said, blushing furiously.

"Why in the world would I need all those? I asked for anything they had in London, which is where Douglas lived."

"I realise that now. I'm sorry. I'll telephone them straightaway and also check what's in the national database. I'll get the reports to you as soon as I can."

She was clearly flustered and embarrassed, and began snatching up the files she'd brought quickly and carelessly in her hurry to be out of the room. Before they knew it, she'd dropped the whole lot on the floor; papers scattered

A Frosty Combination

everywhere and mixed together. Jennifer was horrified and glanced at the look of exasperation on Bonnie's face.

"Look, don't worry about this, I'll take it all through to the interview room and start putting it back together in its proper order," Lilly said to Jennifer. "You make a start on collating what Bonnie needs, then you can take over from me when you've got it all. Okay?"

"Okay, thank you," she replied, opening the door. "Sorry again."

"Thanks, Lilly," Bonnie said, crouching on the floor and starting to help pick up the papers.

"Leave this to me. You just eat your pizza, Bonnie. It shouldn't take me too long to get this sorted out."

"I really need to see about getting this lot transferred to the computer," Bonnie said, picking up a musty smelling file. "Look, this one is twenty years old. I better find a temp from one of the bigger stations who can come in part time and do some data entry for us."

Lilly left with the files while Bonnie was scribbling herself a reminder on a bright pink post-it note, which she stuck on a board above her desk.

※

BY THE TIME she had got to the interview room and spread all the files and papers on the table, Lilly realised she'd seriously underestimated the time it would take to get everything back in order. She took off her coat and hung it on the back of the chair. For once, the old-fashioned Victorian radiator was cranking out a good amount of heat. Albeit noisily, with periodic bangs and hisses, which made her jump until she got used to it.

She started by double checking the files, in between mouthfuls of pizza, which appeared not to have been affected, stacking them in a pile on the floor before laying out all the empty folders with the name and case numbers showing.

"Right, let's see…" she said, grabbing the uppermost loose sheet, which she'd heaped together on the chair. "Anderson…" she eventually found the relevant file and, checking the case number matched, slipped the paper inside. Fifteen minutes later, pizza finished, and only eleven pieces of paper filed in the correct place, Lilly fervently hoped Jennifer was having better luck. If she had to do this on her own, she'd be here all night.

For the next two hours, she worked alone and in silence before Jennifer finally joined her. Looking much less flustered than she had previously.

"I think I've averted a complete disaster! The old London files are being scanned and emailed to Bonnie, and I've managed to print out the more recent stuff from the database which I've already given to her. I can't thank you enough for helping me out of this mess, Lilly."

"Is there a lot to go through?" Lilly asked.

Jennifer shook her head. "Not really, but it takes time to track it all down, especially if it's still in a hard copy format like this lot is," she said, waving her hand over the table.

"Has Bonnie eaten?"

"Yes, she's finished her pizza and was on the phone when I left."

"Good. She forgets to eat when she's working on an investigation like this," Lilly said.

"I've noticed that, too. She works far harder than any of the men. You wouldn't find them skipping meals for the sake of the case. Unfortunately, my clumsiness has made it more difficult."

"It was an accident, Jennifer. It could have happened to anyone. Now, if Bonnie is busy, I'll stay for a while longer and work through this lot with you. Did you find the missing husband, by the way?"

"I sent a PC round to take a statement from the wife. It turns out he did come home from the pub after all, but rather than face the wrath of his other half, he slept in the garden shed all night. Our constable found him sleeping on a camp bed and snoring his head off. It's obviously a well-used bolt hole for him to escape from his spouse."

While she'd been talking, Jennifer had pulled up the second chair and got stuck into the filing. It moved along much faster now there were two of them.

Lilly stuck several more sheets into their corresponding folders before picking up one she stopped to read. It belonged to a man called Clive Barnard. According to the latest report, he was spending the last years of his life in prison for the murder of his girlfriend twelve years earlier.

"I didn't realise there were so many domestic abuse cases in and around Plumpton Mallet," Lilly said sadly.

"It's dreadful isn't it?" Jennifer said. "You never really know what people are going through behind closed doors, and domestic abuse victims are adept at putting on a brave face and hiding the damage to the world outside. They've usually been beaten down so much over an extended period of time that they truly believe they're worthless and everything is their fault. They live in constant fear of doing or saying something wrong, which will result in severe punishment. They've simply got no strength or self-esteem left with which to fight. It makes me so angry. Although we do have a very high rate of abusers being found guilty and serving time here, regrettably, that's not the case everywhere. Personally, I'd like to see them all shipped off to some penal colony somewhere along with all the other undesirables. Let them damage each other away from civilised society."

The Barnard case had stood out to Lilly simply because of the victim's name, Janet Scott. It was the same surname as one of her employees, and she wondered if there was a family connection. Scanning the loose reports, she came across the transcript for the original 999 call. It had been Janet's fifteen-year-old son who had made the call.

"Oh, no..." she said, covering her mouth and feeling sick. Suddenly, his behavior and reactions to Monty made sense.

"What is it?" Jennifer asked, concern etched on her pretty face.

"I've just found this file from twelve years ago," Lilly said. "This man, Clive Barnard, killed his girlfriend. She was the mother of one of my employees. I had no idea he'd gone through something as dreadful as this. No wonder Monty's abuse of Abigail struck such a chord with him."

"Poor man," Jennifer said, studying the details. "He was just fifteen."

Lilly nodded, not trusting herself to speak. She tucked the loose sheets back in the file and set it to one side. As much as it pained her, she needed to show it to Bonnie.

She helped Jennifer collate a few more files, then headed back to Bonnie's office. She was on yet another telephone call, so she took a seat and waited.

"Sorry about that, Lilly. I've just been informed there will be a delay in getting those files from London. There's a power outage apparently which means no internet, and that means no files. They are working on it, but I'm not holding my breath that I'll get anything soon. Honestly, if it isn't one thing, it's another. So, how are you getting on with the files?"

"We've broken the back of it. It's not difficult, just time consuming. But that's not what I wanted to talk to you about. I came across this," she said, waving the file. "It's a domestic case where the woman was killed by her boyfriend."

Bonnie nodded. "It's not uncommon, I'm afraid, Lilly. What's special about this one?"

"Look at the name of the victim and who it was who called the police."

Bonnie took the file and opened it. "Ah, I see. Poor kid."

"His mother was murdered, and he found the body, Bonnie. He was only fifteen. Still at school."

"Tragic," murmured Bonnie. "But how do you feel it connects to Monty's murder?"

"I don't know. It probably doesn't, but I thought you should know."

"Well, I'm certainly not dismissing it. There's a possible motive now, due to his previous experience, although it's a bit tenuous. Especially considering it was well over a decade ago. Thanks for bringing it to my attention. I'll bear it in mind during the course of my investigation. Although I hope it comes to nothing. I like him."

"Yes, I do too."

Realising the time, Lilly said goodbye to Bonnie and made her way back out into the cold. Darkness had fallen, the temperature had plummeted and a sharp wind was whirling around the town as she made her way back to the shop. Luckily, the street lamps and the many Christmas lights helped her negotiate the slippery pavements.

The shop was closed and the lights off in Stacey's apartment, but a single bulb shone from the lamp at the back of the shop. She unlocked the door and immediately Earl Grey bounded from his warm, cosy bed and began purring loudly while rubbing himself against her ankles. She scooped him up, gave him a hug, then put him in his carrier, knowing Stacey would have fed him before she left. Making sure everything was locked up, she turned off the lamp and exited through the rear door to her car.

It was a steady drive home, but eventually she was pulling up outside her cottage. Inside she gave Earl an extra treat of tuna which, much to her amusement, he ate slowly and delicately, almost as though he was a restaurant critic, savouring every mouthful in order to write a report afterwards. He washed his paws and whiskers thoroughly, then retired to his bed. She made a cup of chamomile tea for herself, taking it through to the cosy lounge. She needed something to calm the knot of anxiety in her stomach.

If the person whose name was in those files had murdered Monty, it would be a severe blow to everyone she knew, but especially to Stacey. She was the reason he was working at the Tea Emporium in the first place. She gazed into the flames of the fire, thinking deeply about the case. Monty had undoubtedly made enemies everywhere he went, but could it really be one of her friends who had killed him? She felt nauseous at the possibility and made a mental note to phone Bonnie tomorrow to see if she'd received the files from London. Hopefully, there would be something in those that would give them a new lead to investigate. She fell asleep on the sofa, her dreams plagued with murder.

Chapter Twelve

*E*ARLY THE NEXT morning, Lilly received an excited text message from Rodney telling her he'd finished developing all the photos from the Christmas Market. He was obviously very eager to show her and as it was his day off, she suggested she come to his house to see them. He sent a text in reply saying she'd be very welcome.

He'd refused any sort of compensation for his time and cost of materials when Lilly had offered, so after a quick call to Stacey explaining what she was doing, she quickly baked two small batches of scones to give him as a thank you. The first was a savoury with cheese and chive and the other a sweet version using a colourful mixture of dried fruit.

At the shop, she dropped Earl off and also picked up some of Rodney's favourite teas to take with her, along with two take out cups, one for each of them. "I shouldn't be too long," she told Stacey. "I'm looking forward to seeing the pictures."

"Trust me, they'll be awesome," Stacey said enthusiastically. "He has a real eye for photography. It's a pity you missed his last exhibition. It was incredible. I'll take you to his next one, though."

"I'll look forward to it. You'll be okay here for an hour or so?"

Stacey told her she'd be fine handling the shop now her dad was back at her side, helping her. Which reminded Lilly she needed to check with Bonnie about the reports she'd received from London. Assuming they'd arrived. She knew how busy her police detective friend was so doubted she'd had a chance to go through the information yet, even if it had all been sent over. She decided to go to the station after she'd been to see Rodney and informed Stacey of her plan. There must be some answers there.

Lilly left as James was helping a newly arrived customer and Stacey was dusting the shelves. She smiled. It was good to see them together again. They made an excellent team, and she knew she was leaving the shop in good hands.

Rodney lived on the outskirts of Plumpton Mallet, much like herself, but in the opposite direction. It was a semi-detached home built of old stone, with a bay window looking onto a small patch of garden fronted by an evergreen privet hedge, now topped with snow. She parked on the road outside, the drive being taken up by Rodney's car, and opening the wrought-iron gate, walked down the stone path and rang the doorbell. He answered almost immediately.

"Hello, Lilly, welcome. Come in. Is that my favourite tea by any chance?" he asked with a huge grin.

"It is," Lilly replied, stamping the snow off her boots on the doormat and handing him a mug. "I've brought you some boxes of leaves as well, and made you some scones. It's a thank you for doing all the photography work for the shops."

"Oh, that's really great. Thanks, Lilly," he said in surprise. "Come through to the kitchen and we can have one with our tea."

The kitchen was a throwback to the nineteen-eighties. Everything was either beige or brown, including the chocolate coloured plastic washing-up bowl, drainer and brush. It even had an orange pine picnic style table and benches, which Lilly remembered were very popular during the time. She sat on one of the benches and took a buttered cheese scone from Rodney.

"I remember this style of kitchen growing up in the eighties," she said. "My mum and dad had the same units."

Rodney nodded. "I've been thinking of updating it for a while, but I can't bring myself to do it. It was before I was born, but mum saved and saved to get this kitchen and did a lot of the work herself. She was really proud of it."

"She did a very good job," Lilly said.

"She did. She died when I was young."

Lilly didn't want to keep what she already knew from Rodney. "I know. I'm sorry. I came across Clive Barnard's case files when I was helping Bonnie at the police station yesterday."

Rodney immediately tensed. "But that's private information."

"It is, and I didn't mean to pry. There was an accident with the historical files. They were all dropped and got mixed up. I was helping sort them out when I saw your name on the emergency call transcript. I've been worried about you ever since."

"Worried?" he asked, but he could obviously see she was genuinely concerned about him. "Lilly, it was a long time ago. It's pointless worrying about it all now."

"I know, but it must have been incredibly traumatic for you. You were so young. I thought perhaps what happened between Monty and Abigail was opening up old wounds, so wanted to make sure you were all right."

Rodney halved and buttered another scone without speaking, the action giving him time to process what he wanted to say. "I'd be lying if I said it didn't," he admitted, pushing the untouched scone away. "I'm sure you noticed I don't have patience for bullies like him."

"That's why you came to Abigail's defence on Market Day," Lilly said. "You looked as though you were about to give Monty the hiding of a lifetime."

"I probably would have done if Bonnie hadn't got there first. I'm sorry if I've seemed a bit off this last week. Even though it's twelve years since mum died, I'm still angry about what happened. I'm trying to work through some stuff, but I don't think you can ever get over something like that. I've always wondered what my life would have been like if it hadn't happened and mum was still here."

"I understand, Rodney," Lilly said. "You know, I have been seeing an excellent counsellor recently, Dr Jorgenson. He's been helping me work through some divorce related issues, as well as a few other things. I could give you his card if you need someone to talk to."

Rodney nodded. "Okay. Thanks. I didn't know you were married?" he said. "You never talk about it."

Lilly shrugged. "It was a while ago now, and we split amicably. Or so I thought. It turns out I was harbouring some ill will towards my ex-husband, which wasn't healthy." She grabbed a pen and notebook and, writing down the doctor's number, tore out the sheet and gave it to Rodney.

"I was in counselling after mum died," he said. "I didn't have much of a choice at the time because of my age. I don't know if it did any good. Maybe it will help more now. Who knows?"

Lilly could well imagine Rodney being urged by the authorities and the family doctor to undertake a lengthy series of counselling sessions after his mother had been killed. It was the type of trauma which should never be pushed aside. She couldn't imagine what it had been like for him to have lived with his mother, knowing she was being abused yet impotent to help. Then, finding her dead must have shaken him to the core. The recent events must have brought it all to the surface, and she truly hoped he would seek out Dr Jorgenson's help.

"You know I'm here if you ever want to talk, Rodney?" he nodded. Lilly could see he was uncomfortable talking about his mother's death, so changed the subject. "Now, where are those photos you took? I've been looking forward to seeing them."

A Frosty Combination

FROM THE KITCHEN, Rodney led Lilly into the hall where there was a door under the stairs. Like most houses in Plumpton Mallet built over a century ago, this led to the cellar where the kitchen would have been housed in days of old.

She followed him down the flight of stone steps, lit by a single bulb hanging from a wire, and at the bottom turned right along a short corridor. A door with a single unlit bulb above, no doubt turning red when it was in use, led into the dark room. Rodney flicked on the light switch and turned to Lilly with a huge grin.

"This is where the magic happens," he said proudly.

Lilly could see that while Rodney had hardly touched the fixtures and fittings in the main house, down here he'd spared no expense in getting a fully working dark room in order. The small window, set high in the wall, would have looked over the back garden at ground level, but had been boarded over with an air vent set in the middle. In the space within the chimney where a cooking range would have been, there was now open shelving containing boxes of photographic paper. And across the length of one side wall there was a long metal table with a sink and various trays. A large piece of apparatus above the table was on rails, allowing it to be moved from side to side with a large lens pointing down. She had no idea how any of it worked, but as she approached the washing lines strung up across the room, where countless images were hanging with the aid of small wooden pegs, she realised just how innately talented Rodney was.

He had taken some fabulous candid shots of market day, but had also done a series of more arty style ones too. One in particular stood out to Lilly, it was of Laura's glass stall. One of her stunning red ornaments, but he'd caught the reflection of a little blonde girl in a red bobble hat in the snow, wearing a Christmas dress with her tongue out, catching the falling snowflakes. It was worthy of a Sunday supplement.

"Rodney, this is amazing," Lilly said. "I remember this little girl. She asked her mum if she was at the North Pole where Santa lived. She was adorable. I hope you're going to send it to Laura? She'll be absolutely thrilled with it."

Lilly knew the ornament had been one of the few to survive when the stall was damaged, but seeing it like this might just help Laura to continue with her art. She was immensely talented and this could be the boost she needed.

"I've told her about it already," he replied. "That one is probably my favourite from the whole event, but I managed to get some great images of the stalls. Look at this one. I bet you didn't know I'd taken it, did you?"

Lilly took the proffered photograph and discovered it was of her and Abigail, both roaring with laughter as they spoke to several customers. He'd captured them and the whole spirit of the event perfectly.

"It's fantastic, Rodney," Lilly said. "And you're right, I had no idea you'd taken it. I doubt Abigail was aware either."

"I thought it would be perfect as a promotional image. Both the logos are in the background. The Tea Emporium one is very clear, and you can see the phrase Agony Aunt's café between the two of you. I thought it would be a good one for the supplement the Gazette is doing," he said. "And you're both holding the take out mugs. Plus, the array of tea sets and teas in the background means it captured everything."

A Frosty Combination

"Stacey said you had a real eye for photography, but I honestly had no idea you were this good, Rodney. You could get a fantastic job doing this, you know? As a photojournalist, maybe, or in fashion. Maybe travel or sports even. Truly, I think you could have the pick of any job out there based on the small amount I've seen of your portfolio. You could travel the world if you wanted to."

"I've been doing it since I was twelve. I've updated it now, but this was actually my mum's dark room. She did as many jobs as she could to support us, from waitressing and cleaning to taking in other people's washing and ironing. Her career as a photographer, even though she had to keep it secret, was just beginning to take off when she died."

Lilly thought it was wonderful that Rodney had kept up his mother's dream. He had such a natural and instinctive talent that she wouldn't be surprised if he won awards at some point in the future.

She perused the other images hanging on the lines. More pictures of Laura's booth and the tea shop and café. Happy families frolicking in the snow and kids having snowball fights. A close up of a woman holding one of their coffee mugs, the steam rising in swirls, partly obscuring her face while snowflakes fell around her.

Another of Bonnie and Abigail helping an elderly customer who was holding onto a cute Dachshund with a red bow tie round his neck. Arty shots of the bandstand and the musicians. And several of the town lights and the Christmas tree taken from various angles. Children with the animals at the nativity set, and more with Santa in his grotto.

"Your mum would be very proud of you, Rodney," she said.

He nodded. "I hope so."

"Do you think I could take that one of me and Abigail?"

He picked it up and handed it to her. "Of course. I've got the negative so I can print as many as you need."

"I'm going to give it to Archie to go along with the article he's writing. I wouldn't be surprised if you get some offers of work once your name appears as the photographer."

"That would be a welcome bonus. It's quite an expensive hobby," Rodney said. "I suppose having your picture in the paper for something positive, rather than helping with a murder inquiry, will be good for you too."

Lilly started, wholly immersed in the happy images of the Christmas market, she'd almost forgotten someone had been killed.

***

She frowned and put the photograph in her handbag. "I just seem to have a knack for it," she said.

"Are you still helping with the Monty Douglas case?"

"Yes. As much as I can, anyway. I'm worried about James, you see. He's not been cleared even though he's out of jail cell. It's hanging over all of us."

"I wouldn't worry too much, Lilly. The police don't have any real evidence against him to secure a conviction. And there's a lot of other suspects, isn't there? It must be someone from out of town, so I wouldn't be surprised if they never find out who did it."

A Frosty Combination

Lilly continued looking at the other pictures while they talked. "I wonder if your camera caught anything suspicious?"

"I doubt it. I was at the stalls all day and Monty was killed outside your tea shop. I think he must have bought his drink from there because he certainly wouldn't have come back and got it from the stall after what happened."

"I suppose that makes sense. But no one remembers serving him. Someone else could have bought it for him, I suppose, although I can't imagine who. It's not as though he had friends here. However, it doesn't bode well for James if he did get the tea from the shop."

Lilly sighed, more confused than ever and with a tight feeling of pressure just beginning across her forehead, the starts of a tension headache she realised with dismay. Her eyes ranged from the photographs to a shelf in the corner of the room, where she spotted a small steel pocket flask. "Drinking on the job?" she teased, and Rodney smiled.

"Whatever you do, don't drink it," he said. "One of my chemical drums sprung a leak last week, just a small hole, but it's dangerous stuff. I stuck the flask under it to catch the drips until I could mend it."

"I noticed a lot of chemicals in here," Lilly said curiously. "What's it all used for?"

"Developing the photos," Rodney replied, passion in his eyes. "I'm really old school like my mum when it comes to photography."

Lilly's heart began to thump as her eyes quickly scanned the names of the chemicals in the various bottles and canisters, then jumped involuntarily back to the pocket flask. It would have been easy to offer Monty a small tot of whiskey in his tea. He was a known drinker and after the morning he'd had would have welcomed a shot of booze to take the edge off. Could what happened to his mother have made Rodney kill Monty before he hurt Abigail permanently?

No, he was at the Tea Emporium stall the whole time, Lilly thought. *So, that doesn't make sense. When could he have met Monty outside my shop?*

"Well, thanks for showing me around, Rodney. I'm going to get this photo over to Archie before his deadline."

"Of course. I'll show you out. And thanks for the tea and scones."

"You're welcome."

Outside, Lilly went to her car and, after Rodney had disappeared back indoors, made a call to Archie. She wanted to make sure he could include the picture in his write up. She left it ringing a few times, but there was no answer. Ending the call, she sat drumming her fingers on the steering wheel, looking back at the house thoughtfully. Out of all the scenarios she had entertained, this one made the most sense to her. Rodney had lost his mother due to domestic violence. The way Monty had treated Abigail had brought the horrors of his past to the surface and, carrying the guilt of his inability to save his mother, he took the opportunity to save Abigail instead.

But he didn't have the opportunity, Lilly thought again.

She decided to call Bonnie. She wanted to share what she'd learned and talk it through with her. Again, the call was unanswered. "Isn't anyone working today?" she

A Frosty Combination

muttered in frustration, just as the battery in her mobile phone died. "Oh, for heaven's sake," she said, scrabbling around her bag for the charger, only to find it missing. She put her bag on the passenger seat and turned the keys in the ignition. The engine sputtered and whined in a valiant attempt to start, but eventually gave up the ghost altogether. She groaned and rested her head against the steering wheel for a moment.

She was just trying to find the energy and motivation to walk the mile and a half back to town in the freezing cold when Rodney came out of the house. He gave her a quizzical look, and she got out of the car.

"My phone battery has just died and my car won't start. It's probably the cold weather."

"Don't worry, I've got some jump leads handy. I had to use them myself the other day, if you remember? Let's try to get it started that way. If we don't have any luck, I'll drop you off in town."

"That would be great. Thanks, Rodney."

Rodney opened the boot of his car while Lilly stood and waited. She spotted the small container of chemical salts immediately. "What's that?" she asked, trying to sound friendly and unconcerned.

"Oh, just photography stuff. It's about time I took it indoors, actually. I shouldn't leave it in the cold."

"Oh, been there a while, has it?" Lilly said with a brittle laugh that sounded forced even to her own ears. "I'm always forgetting to take stuff out of my car."

Rodney shrugged. "A couple of weeks. I'd forgotten I'd bought it."

A couple of weeks? Lilly thought, as Rodney held up the jump leads and moved to pop the bonnet of her car. *That means the chemicals were in his car on market day. But when could he have seen Monty at the shop when he was working on the stall?*

Then she suddenly remembered Archie's tea set. Archie had bought the set for his cousin and Rodney had taken it back to the shop for him to keep it safe. He was there! Her heart was racing as Rodney asked her to turn on her engine and rev the accelerator. Her hands were shaking as she tried to turn the key.

"Are you all right, Lilly?" Rodney asked.

"Fine, just cold," she said, trying to think what she could do. Her phone was dead, her car didn't work, and she knew without a shadow of a doubt that Rodney knew she was onto him. She gave him a smile, thinking it might help.

He eyed her for a moment, and then turned to look back at his own car. The container of Sodium Cyanide crystals was available for all to see. He let out a loud sigh and moved towards her. Not wanting to be trapped in her car, she hurriedly got out and stepped away from him.

"HE DESERVED IT, Lilly," Rodney said softly. Lilly shook her head. "I don't know what you mean, Rodney," she said in an attempt to feign innocence, but it was clearly too late. He took another step towards her and she scrabbled back, her boots refusing to gain purchase on the icy path. She grabbed the roof of the car and managed to stay upright.

"You've been very good to me, Lilly. But I'm not giving up. I've come too far and done too much to stop now."

"Giving up? Done too much?" Lilly squeaked. She had no idea what he meant, but couldn't afford to waste time thinking about it. Her mind raced as she tried desperately to think of a way out of this perilous situation. Maybe she could talk him into turning himself in? She doubted it would work, but she had to try something.

"James won't go to jail, you know?" Rodney said. "They can't pin this murder on him, or me, or anyone else, for that matter. You have to trust me, Lilly. It's all going to be fine. But I have to trust you too."

"Rodney, I don't understand. What do you mean?"

"I'm going to get rid of them all, Lilly. The world doesn't need people like Monty. They shouldn't be allowed to ruin people's lives," he said, just as a car turned into the road in the distance. Rodney briefly glanced behind him, then turned back and gave her a venomous look. "I thought you would understand. I haven't finished my work, but you called the police."

"I... I didn't," Lilly stammered. "I promise. My phone battery died," almost gasping with relief at the sight of Bonnie's car. She needed to keep him talking just a moment longer.

"You can't tell the police or it will all have been for nothing," Rodney said now, panic in his eyes. "I told you, I'm getting rid of them all and I can't let you get in the way, Lilly. I'm sorry, but I just can't."

Lilly barely had time to wonder who the 'all' was before Rodney launched himself at her. She sprinted round the rear of her car, and with immense luck it was Rodney who slipped and fell on the ice, giving her a minuscule head start. She bolted down the street toward the police car, feet slipping and sliding and arms wind-milling furiously in an attempt to keep herself upright. Rodney hot on her heels. He was faster though and she couldn't compete. He caught up with her in the middle of the road, just as Bonnie slammed on her brakes, nearly spinning out of control on the ice to avoid hitting them. He grabbed the hood of her coat, pulling her roughly toward him, but Bonnie was out of the car yelling at him to release her before his grip had even begun to tighten. He let go and raised his hands.

"They will thank me when this is all over, you know?" he shouted. "I'm eradicating the disease. Cutting out the tumour."

"Bonnie, he killed Monty."

Bonnie didn't question Lilly, just yelled at Rodney to lie on the ground, hands behind his head. She snapped on a pair of handcuffs, then unceremoniously dragged him to the car, forced him in the back seat and slammed the door. Only then did she turn to her friend.

"Are you all right, Lilly?"

"Bonnie, how did you know where I was?" Lilly asked.

"I was having coffee with Archie, talking about the case, when we both noticed we'd got missed calls from you. You didn't answer when we called you back and we got a bit concerned. I called the shop and Stacey said you were here. I had a feeling something wasn't right, so I drove over. That, and the pathologist report named photography as a possible field where the poison could be used."

Lilly smiled. "I am so glad you came, Bonnie."

"So, Rodney killed Monty? How do you know? Has he confessed to you?"

"Almost, but he wasn't making a lot of sense. You'll need to come and have a look in his car and his house. I can explain how I know better that way. Just so we're clear, Bonnie, I didn't come to question him about the murder. I came to look at the market day photos."

"I believe you," Bonnie said.

"Bonnie, Rodney was saying some really strange things which I didn't understand. That his work wasn't finished, he was 'getting rid of them all,' and 'eradicating the disease,' 'cutting out the tumour.' Do you know what he meant?"

Bonnie's face drained of colour as she stared at Rodney in the back of her car. "Oh, my God," she said. "I think I do know. Jennifer dug up some very interesting information last night. I need a team here. Let me make call then we can talk. It looks as though we have a lot to share with one other."

Chapter Thirteen

A WEEK TO THE day later, on Thursday 23rd of December, it was time for the staff Christmas party. It was being hosted in the newly opened tea room in the Agony Aunt's café. Lilly and Abigail had spent the last two evenings after both businesses had closed, decorating it with all manner of trimmings. Including what appeared to be several miles of tinsel. Abigail, it seemed, had a real love for the stuff. There was also an enormous Christmas tree that everyone had pitched in to decorate by purchasing as many glass ornaments from Laura as she had available. It had helped her out enormously with her expenses, and now the tree was glistening with all manner of decorative glass, making it a stunning focal point for the room.

Lilly had also heard that all the other vendors from the Christmas market had organised a whip round for her. The money was nearly enough to pay off her debts. No doubt she would be back next year with a stall brimming with beautiful glass.

A medley of Christmas music was playing on the brand new music system and both the café and the tea shop had closed early for the party. Those who hadn't been scheduled to work that day were arriving in their best Christmas outfits. Others had either dashed home to get ready or had used the staff changing room, having brought their outfits with them. Everyone had glasses of eggnog, champagne, and wine. Or in the case of those being sensible and pacing themselves, mostly the older crowd, peppermint and cranberry tea or Abigail's hot orange chocolate. Lilly had also set up a fully equipped cocktail table with recipes printed out for them to mix themselves. The younger members of the team were already having immense fun with it.

Stacey had surprised Lilly and Abigail with fake snow and washable window paint to decorate the windows in both the café and the tea shop, and had done a snow scene with children sledging down a hill to a waiting Santa Claus with a sledge full of presents. Abigail had decorated each table with Christmas themed cloths and battery operated candles, which looked remarkably real. Hanging above the doorway was a bunch of mistletoe, which, much to everyone's amusement, Stacey and Fred had immediately made use of.

The kitchen staff had all been given time off to attend, so Abigail and Lilly were now bringing out the party food they'd made themselves. Miniature sausage rolls, sausages and cheese on sticks, huge platters of sandwiches, miniature quiches, vol-au-vents and several deserts including sherry trifle and raspberry Pavlova, now filled the buffet table.

Lilly was just adding the last plate of mince pies dusted with icing sugar to the table, an English Christmas tradition which Stacey couldn't get enough of when she was informed that Archie and Bonnie had arrived. She hurried over to the door. Bonnie was carrying a large gift-wrapped box, and Archie a small envelope with a copy of tomorrow's paper.

"Is that it?" Lilly asked eagerly, reaching out for the newspaper.

"It is indeed," Archie replied.

Lilly had been waiting for Archie's latest article. They had discussed it between them and decided rather than re-hash the previous awful news which Archie had already written about, they wanted to highlight the positive results which had developed after Rodney had been arrested. It was rare, but sometimes good things came from bad deeds. This was one of those times.

Once Archie and Bonnie had placed their gifts under the tree, Lilly took the paper to one of the banquettes and put it on the table. The front-page headline read, *"The Positive Side of Murder."* With the subtitle, *"Local Agony Aunts and Poisoner join forces to support Women's Shelter."*

"Great title," Fred said over Lilly's shoulder.

Lilly had sat down and the entire staff had gathered round her. "Read it out loud, Lilly," Jean said, temporarily turning off the music.

"All right," Lilly said and took a deep breath.

A Frosty Combination

Lilly Tweed and Abigail Douglas never expected their small town businesses would become involved in a murder investigation, let alone that the astute Miss Tweed would once again play such a vital role in solving the case with great risk to her personal wellbeing. But the investigation into the Plumpton Mallet Christmas Market murder that took the life of Mrs Douglas' former spouse, Montgomery, has taken an interesting, and dare we say positive, turn of events.

During the market less than two weeks ago, Monty Douglas was found dead outside the Tea Emporium, owned and operated by Miss Tweed. This launched an investigation by the local police that, for a brief spell, had them baffled. With Mr Douglas' colourful history of domestic violence and a tendency to leave the lives of former friends in shambles, there was a slew of suspects for Detective Bonnie Phillips to sift through.

With the help of Lilly Tweed, the police were led to the door of student and amateur photographer Rodney Scott. A former employee of the Agony Aunt's Lilly Tweed and Abigail Douglas, Scott poisoned the victim's drink, allegedly tricking him into believing a flask he carried contained whiskey when, in fact, it was filled with a toxic chemical used in his photography hobby.

Scott has since confessed to the murder of Montgomery Douglas, but during the course of several interviews, his comments, combined with a discovery made by one of the staff at the station, convinced Detective Phillips to dig further.

"You didn't mention Jennifer?" Bonnie interrupted, addressing Archie.

"She asked me not to name her," Archie said.

"Really? Why?"

"She said it was only by dint of her clumsiness that you discovered there was more to the story. She said she could hardly take credit for an accident."

Bonnie shook her head. "Silly girl. Okay, carry on, Lilly."

"Continued on page three," Lilly said, turning the page over and clearing her throat.

Upon further investigation, Detective Phillips discovered a connection between Scott and a missing person's case, which had gone cold. William Barr, a resident of a nearby town, vanished several months ago, but over recent days Scott has confessed to the murder and led the police to the spot where he disposed of the body. Barr was a known wife beater.

From what this reporter has managed to learn, Rodney Scott had proposed to take the lives of several known abusers within the area, and had he not been caught intended to expand his activity to the neighbouring counties and beyond.

After searching Scott's home Detective Phillips and her crime team discovered in-depth information and meticulous plans to murder over two dozen men with a history of domestic abuse and violence, one of whom had been assaulted four weeks prior outside a local pub but had managed to fend off his attacker. The perpetrator had never been found. However, Rodney Scott has since admitted to being responsible.

Scott's mother was a victim of domestic abuse, and the young boy found her lifeless body at the tender age of fifteen. This was the root cause of his vigilantism upon reaching adulthood. He's admitted to never having got over her death and his severe feelings of inadequacy at being unable to prevent it. He himself was a victim of prolonged abuse at the hands of the man who killed his mother.

Shortly after his arrest, Scott reached out to his former employers regarding an initiative to provide a positive outcome from so much death. Since then Tweed and Douglas have been exhibiting Scott's photographs, selling them and donating the proceeds to a women's refuge. The new organisation, currently waiting on formal charitable status, which is expected in the New Year, is being led by Tom Livingstone and supported by both Tweed and Douglas, as well as Scott.

Since its formation less than a week ago, 'From Negative to Positive,' has managed to raise over ten thousand pounds for women's shelters across the county from a combination of sales and donations.

While the actions of Rodney Scott are undoubtedly deplorable, it is hoped this new initiative will continue well into the future by raising awareness of what is, in Scott's own words, "A sickness within our society."

- Article by Archie Brown.

There was a momentary silence once Lilly had finished reading, and then everyone broke into spontaneous applause, causing Archie to blush from the roots of his hair. Stacey hugged him fiercely. "It's really good, Archie," she said, dashing a tear from her eye.

"That poor boy," Abigail said, shaking her head. "I obviously don't condone what he did, but it's undeniable that something broke inside him when he found his mother. He'd been through so much as a youngster it's hardly surprising he snapped."

Lilly folded the paper and put it behind the counter, while Jean turned the music back and the party began in earnest. Several people stopped to pat Archie on the back and congratulate him on a great article.

As the party continued, Lilly eventually found Archie alone by the Christmas tree, nursing a Christmas Spirit cocktail with a cherry on a stick and a green umbrella.

"You did such a good job with that write up, Archie. I'm glad you didn't make Rodney the villain of the piece. What will happen to him, do you think?"

"He'll never be free, Lilly, but his solicitor is pushing hard for him to be placed permanently in a psychiatric facility rather than in a normal prison. He wouldn't survive mixing with the general populace, and being put in solitary confinement, I think it would break his spirit completely.

A Frosty Combination

The solicitor has already obtained statements and extensive reports from several experts in the medical community who have interviewed Rodney at length. I, for one, hope he succeeds. Rodney was failed by the system too, you know. He was lucky to get out of that hellish situation alive. I hope no one forgets that."

"I hope so too," Lilly said. "Do you think it will happen? That he'll spend his life in a secure hospital, I mean?"

Archie nodded. "Yes, I really do. It's the right thing, Lilly. But if by some cruel fate it doesn't, then I'll use all of my investigative power and means at my disposal to lobby hard to make it happen."

"You're a good egg, Archie Brown," Lilly said, giving him a hug. "I'm very proud to call you my friend."

They were interrupted then by Bonnie staggering in under the weight of a magnificent Christmas cake, decorated in royal icing and topped with two small figurines dressed in festive clothing. It was obvious to everyone as they crowded round they were miniatures of Lilly and Abigail, each holding a sign for the Tea Emporium and The Agony Aunt's café, respectively.

"Bonnie!" exclaimed Lilly. "That's incredible. When on earth did you find time to make that?"

Bonnie rolled her eyes and, with assistance from Archie, placed the cake on the buffet table. "You've obviously had too much eggnog, Lilly, since when have you ever known me to bake anything? Especially not something as professional as this. Susanna at The Loafer did it for me, which is a good thing because it would have been inedible if I'd done it. Happy Christmas everyone. Now, who wants a slice?"

It turned out everybody did, so a large knife was found from the kitchen and Bonnie did the honours, having first removed the figures and presented them to their living counterparts. Archie patted his stomach and pronounced himself too full to eat another bite after the buffet, then promptly took a slice and made it disappear faster than a magician. Lilly laughed. It was such a good feeling to be celebrating among friends. She glanced over to where James was sitting happily, deep in conversation with both Stacey and Fred. Fred made a comment and James laughed and patted him on the shoulder. Lilly nodded. They'd all be fine.

Soon the time came for the Secret Santa exchange.

"Who had Rodney?" Stacey asked sadly.

"I did," Abigail said. "Unfortunately, I wasn't able to return or exchange it. But never mind, perhaps I can learn to use it myself."

"What did you get him?" James asked.

"A new camera."

"Wow, Abigail, that must have cost a fortune," Stacey said. "You know there was a cap on the amount, right?"

"Yes, but I knew he didn't have much and his other one was so old."

Archie leaned forward. "Would you be willing to sell it to me, Abigail?" he said softly. "I could do with a new one."

Abigail looked at him in surprise. "Are you sure, Archie?"

Archie nodded and Lilly thought, *look who is warming to Abigail finally.* The other gifts were beginning to be handed round, so she found her gift basket and, making her way through the sea of bodies, presented it to James. "Merry Christmas, James."

A Frosty Combination

"Oh, thank you, Lilly," he said, tearing off the paper.

Once the basket of goodies was unwrapped, he laughed uproariously at all the American themed knick-knacks she'd managed to find. There were also some lovely history books in the mix and a small Uncle Sam teddy bear waving two flags. Then his eyes caught sight of the glass Chrysler Building paperweight nestled safely in the middle. "Where did you get this?" he asked, his voice choked with emotion.

"I commissioned Laura to make it. Is it close to the one you had?"

He nodded. "Very close," he said, and gave her a grateful smile. "Lilly... thank you. This really does mean a lot. I can't believe you remembered."

"Dad, it's just the Chrysler building," Stacey said, unaware of the significance.

James laughed and patted her knee affectionately. "It's much more than that, Stacey. I'll tell you all about it later."

As the music changed to a Christmas Conga, everyone formed a line and began kicking their legs and snaking around the tables. Lilly found herself at the door with a special cocktail Fred had just invented and named 'White Christmas.' She took one mouthful and spluttered. "Crikey, a bit too much white rum, I think," she said to herself, wiping her eyes and putting the glass down on the nearest table. She'd almost pulled herself together when Archie joined her.

"Are you all right? You look a bit red in the face."

"I am now, but if Fred offers you a White Christmas cocktail, don't accept. It's lethal."

"Noted. Well, I can finally reveal that you're my Secret Santa recipient, Miss Tweed," he said, and delving in his inside pocket, brought forth a bright red envelope. "I hope you like it."

"I'm sure I will," she said, ripping open the envelope. "Oh, my gosh, Archie," she breathed in wonderment as she discovered what was inside.

Two tickets for the Steam Dream. A luxury travel experience on a Steam Train to the lakes. "Carriages with elegant wood panelling, vintage table lamps, curtains, luxury armchair seating, and Pullman Style dining evocative of a bygone era," she read aloud.

"I thought it would be nice for us both to go," Archie said. "You and I hardly spend time together like we used to."

"I can't think of anything more perfect, Archie. It's something I've always wanted to do. I truly can't wait. Thank you so much."

He nodded, quickly brushed her lips with his own, then, giving a most uncharacteristic blush, muttered something about a drink and left. Lilly was left wondering what on earth had just happened? She glanced up, suddenly remembering the sprig of mistletoe above the door.

"Well I never. Archie Brown," she said softly as several thousand excited butterflies began to dance in her stomach.

If you enjoyed *A Frosty Combination*, the fifth book in the Tea & Sympathy series, please leave a review on Amazon. It really does help other readers find the books.

ABOUT THE AUTHOR

J. New is the author of *THE YELLOW COTTAGE VINTAGE MYSTERIES,* traditional English whodunits with a twist, set in the 1930's. Known for their clever humour as well as the interesting slant on the traditional murder mystery, they have all achieved Bestseller status on Amazon.

J. New also writes two contemporary cozy crime series:

THE TEA & SYMPATHY series featuring Lilly Tweed, former newspaper Agony Aunt now purveyor of fine teas at The Tea Emporium in the small English market town of Plumpton Mallet. Along with a regular cast of characters, including Earl Grey the shop cat.

THE FINCH & FISCHER series featuring mobile librarian Penny Finch and her rescue dog Fischer. Follow them as they dig up clues and sniff out red herrings in the six villages and hamlets that make up Hampsworthy Downs.

Jacquie was born in West Yorkshire, England. She studied art and design and after qualifying began work as an interior designer, moving onto fine art restoration and animal portraiture before making the decision to pursue her lifelong ambition to write. She now writes full time and lives with her partner of twenty-two years, her dog Oscar and twelve cats, all of whom she rescued.

If you would like to be kept up to date with new releases from J. New, you can sign up to her *Reader's Group* on her website www.jnewwrites.com where you will also receive a link to download the free e-book, *The Yellow Cottage Mystery*, the short-story prequel to The Yellow Cottage Vintage Mystery series.

Printed in Great Britain
by Amazon